'As I said, I need to be in London for a few months and your practice has a great reputation.'

Despite her racing heart, Cassie held Leith's gaze. He was bound to question her motives for applying for this job—either suspecting her of exploiting their past relationship in order to secure a position in the well-respected, lucrative practice or—her colour deepened—to see him again. Neither could be further from the truth. It was just one of those unfortunate coincidences that the only job on offer within her particular time-frame was this one, and she desperately, *desperately* needed it. So it didn't matter what he thought. He'd find out soon enough that she had no intention of picking up where they'd left off.

If only he would stop looking at her the way she remembered so well, with his emerald-green eyes unreadable and searching at the same time. It still felt as if he could see into her head.

Dear Reader

As my readers will know, I've written about damaged heroes and heroines who find themselves in heartbreaking and traumatic medical situations. This time I wanted to write about a heroine who has post-traumatic stress disorder and her journey to happiness—and so Cassie was created.

Cassie has had a difficult childhood. Taken away at an early age from her drug-addicted mother and adopted by a couple who don't love her, she's grown up striving for perfection, doubting that anyone can love her for ever.

All that got her through her lonely childhood and teenage years was a burning desire to become a children's doctor.

When she meets Dr Leith Ballantyne, Cassie begins to dream that perhaps she can have her fairytale ending after all—until she discovers that the man she is falling in love with has a son. Not trusting that she can be a good mother to any child because of her own childhood experiences, she decides the best thing she can do for Leith and his son is walk away.

However it seems that fate has different plans for her when she finds herself working with Leith once more, and she is drawn not just to him but to his unhappy little boy.

I have indulged my love of travel in this book—the hero and heroine meet on the Mercy Ship in Africa, are reunited in London, visit Leith's childhood home on the Isle of Skye and fall in love all over again in the Caribbean.

I hope you enjoy Leith and Cassie's story.

Anne Fraser

CINDERELLA OF HARLEY STREET

BY
ANNE FRASER

First published in Great Britain 2013
by Mills & Boon, an imprint of Harlequin (UK) Limited.
Large Print edition 2013
Harlequin (UK) Limited, Eton House,
18-24 Paradise Road, Richmond, Surrey TW9 1SR

© Anne Fraser 2013

ISBN: 978 0 263 23135 9

Anne Fraser was born in Scotland, but brought up in South Africa. After she left school she returned to the birthplace of her parents, the remote Western Islands of Scotland. She left there to train as a nurse, before going on to university to study English Literature. After the birth of her first child she and her doctor husband travelled the world, working in rural Africa, Australia and Northern Canada. Anne still works in the health sector. To relax, she enjoys spending time with her family, reading, walking and travelling.

For Flora, with love and thanks.

Recent titles by Anne Fraser:

HER MOTHERHOOD WISH**
THE FIREBRAND WHO UNLOCKED HIS HEART
MISTLETOE, MIDWIFE…MIRACLE BABY
DOCTOR ON THE RED CARPET
THE PLAYBOY OF HARLEY STREET
THE DOCTOR AND THE DEBUTANTE
DAREDEVIL, DOCTOR…DAD!†
MIRACLE: MARRIAGE REUNITED
SPANISH DOCTOR, PREGNANT MIDWIFE*

**The Most Precious Bundle of All*
†St Piran's Hospital*
The Brides of Penhally Bay

CHAPTER ONE

CASSIE HEAVED HER bag along the quayside, feeling unbearably hot in the midday African sun.

She stopped to rest her aching arms and glanced upwards. The boat was enormous—far bigger than she could ever have imagined. That was good. It would mean that there would be plenty of corners for her to hide in. Naturally she'd socialise whenever it was necessary, but she needed to know that there were places, apart from her cabin, where she could be alone. It wasn't that she didn't like people, she simply preferred her own company.

Her attention was caught by a man standing next to the rail, talking on his phone. Just as Cassie looked up at him he turned his head and for a moment their eyes locked. Her head spun as the strangest sensations twirled around her lower abdomen.

It wasn't as if he was particularly good-looking—

God knew, she had been out with men better looking in her life—but it was the way he carried himself, the tilt of his head, the slight smile on his lips, the way his eyes creased at the corners. If she didn't know differently, she would have sworn she was experiencing simple, pure lust.

When he tipped his head to the side and raised one eyebrow, she flushed, knowing she had been staring. Now a deeper shade of red would be added to the beetroot colour she must already be from heat and exertion. Great. In those few seconds they had held each other's gazes, all sorts of warning bells had gone off in her head. She decided instantly that whoever he was she'd do her best to ignore him in the coming weeks.

She was halfway up the gangway when disaster struck. Her over-filled, slightly battered and definitely seen-better-days suitcase decided it had had enough of being stuffed to the gills, and it exploded, showering her path with T-shirts, dresses and, most embarrassingly, her underwear. She watched with horror as a pair of her lace and silk panties, which had cost her more money than she cared to remember, flew over the handrail, snagged on a piece of metal and fluttered there like some sort of lacy flag of surrender.

Mortified, Cassie lunged for them and almost toppled into the sea. And that was exactly what would have happened had she not found herself caught and held fast against a broad, hard chest.

For the briefest of moments she stayed there. There was something achingly secure about being held in these particular arms.

Which was ridiculous. She didn't need a man—anyone—to make her feel safe.

Somehow she wasn't surprised when she reluctantly extricated herself from the stranger's arms to find that the man who had saved her from falling overboard was the same one who only moments earlier had caught her staring. So much for her promise to herself to avoid him.

'I know it's hot, but I wouldn't recommend the side of the ship for a dip.'

His accent was Scottish, warm and rich with a musical cadence of laughter.

When she looked up at him—he was a good few inches taller than she was—she was horrified to discover that he had rescued her panties and was now holding the flimsy piece of silk and lace in his hands.

'Yours, I believe?' he said with a cheeky grin.

Could her introduction to the ship and the staff get any worse than this? Cassie thought despairingly, noticing that several people were now lining the rails of the ship taking an unabashed interest in what was going on below them. To make matters worse, a group of locals had also stopped and were chattering away to one another in loud, cheerful voices while pointing to Cassie and giggling.

'Thank you,' she said stiffly, grabbing her panties. Really, was there any need for him to hold them up for all to see?

She crouched down and quickly scooped up her scattered belongings, shoving them into the suitcase. Normally, when she packed, everything was perfectly arranged, each item in its place, each T-shirt, skirt, dress and pair of trousers laid on top of each other in graduating colours. Although she knew it was a little obsessional, Cassie liked order—more than liked it, needed it. But unless she wanted to have every item of her wardrobe examined in minute detail there was nothing for it but to get the damn things back in the suitcase and out of sight as quickly as possible. She would have to wait until she reached her cabin before she could sort it all.

Her helper—she refused to think of him as rescuer; it wasn't really an appropriate term for a man who'd mostly retrieved her underwear— crouched down in the confined space of the gangway, so close she could feel the heat radiating from him. The sensation was so intense it robbed her of her breath. However, any attempt to move away would result in her going for the swim he'd joked about. Even if, right now, it was almost tempting.

'I can manage, thank you,' she said. 'I'm sure there are other places you need to be.'

'There are, but I'm pretty sure none of them are quite as entertaining.'

She glanced up at him and again there was that odd frisson running down her spine. She shoved the remaining clothes into her suitcase and almost immediately realised if she tried to close it, first, she would have to sit on it on the steep gangway and, second, even if she did get it closed there was every chance it would burst open again before she could reach her cabin.

It appeared as if the same thought had struck him. He picked up her suitcase, snapped it shut with a single easy movement and tucked it under his arm. 'Deck and cabin number?' he asked. 'At least, I'm assuming you are joining the ship as staff?'

Cassie studied him for a moment. He was tall, almost six-four, she guessed, with sun-lightened brown hair and a wide, full mouth that turned up more at one side than the other. But it was his eyes, an unusual shade of green that drew her. She had the uncanny feeling he could see right into her, see all her secrets, and the sensation wasn't a welcome one.

She became aware that he was waiting for her response with a quizzical smile on his face. 'Dr Ross. Cassie Ross,' she said, holding out her hand.

His smile widened. 'Dr Leith Ballantyne. Welcome to the African Mercy Ship.'

Damn—he was one of the doctors. That would make him difficult to avoid. But, with a bit of luck, he himself would be leaving soon. Cassie had been told that although the nurses tended to stay for a minimum of three months, most of the doctors held permanent jobs elsewhere and, like her, only usually managed to give a few weeks of their time in any one year.

At the top of the gangway she reached for her suitcase. 'I'll take it now, if you don't mind.'

'No. I insist. You must be tired from travelling.' He raised an eyebrow in question. 'London?'

'Yes,' she responded tersely. Then, realising she was being rude, she added, 'Seems days since I left England. I must have experienced every form of transport Africa has to offer over the last forty-eight hours. It's great to finally be here.'

'It's an excellent ship with an excellent team.'

'And I'm looking forward to getting stuck in this afternoon.'

'There'll be no work for you until tomorrow.' Without waiting for her reply, he headed off down a narrow corridor, still holding her suitcase, and she was forced to follow him.

'I'll be fine once I have a shower,' she said to his back.

He turned round. 'Believe me, you'll have enough to do while you're here. How long are you staying anyway?'

'Just over two weeks.'

'Then take the rest while you can. You're going to need it.' When he gave her a lopsided smile she had the crazy sensation of not being able to breathe. She dragged her eyes away from his, hoping he would put the heat in her cheeks down to the sun.

'Perhaps we could have dinner later and I could explain how it works around here?' he continued.

She hadn't been here five minutes and already he was hitting on her. Normally that wouldn't bother her—she'd dealt with men like him plenty of times before, usually brushing them off with a light-hearted quip—but there was something about Leith that disturbed her usual composure.

'I'd like to get to work straight away,' she replied stiffly.

Immediately the laconic manner was gone. 'It's not going to happen. A tired doctor is a dangerous doctor. You are forbidden from working until you've had a good night's sleep.' Then he smiled again. 'So, dinner? It's not haute cuisine, I'm afraid, but it serves its purpose.'

Just who did he think he was, telling her what she could and could not do? She was about to open her mouth to say as much when he swung round and carried on walking. He opened the door to her tiny cabin and dropped her bag on the narrow bunk. There was barely room to swing a cat and she was acutely aware of him standing just a few feet from her.

'I can take it from here,' she said quickly. 'If I can't work, I think I'll skip dinner and have an early night. Now, if you'll excuse me, I think I should find the showers.'

'They're at the end of the corridor.' As he stepped towards her she backed away. She didn't want to be any closer to him than she was already. Annoyingly her pulse was still beating a tattoo in her temples. It had to be the heat.

He grinned again, amusement glinting in his deep green eyes as if he'd noticed her instant reaction to him and it hadn't surprised him. 'If you change your mind about dinner, I'll be in the canteen about seven.'

When he left, Cassie closed the door of her

cabin and sank down on the bed. If at all possible, she was going to avoid Dr Leith Ballantyne.

Leith was whistling as he made his way to his cabin. From the moment he'd first clapped eyes on her, he'd known that life was going to get way more interesting. He normally preferred women with long hair but Cassie's short silky black bob suited her heart-shaped, delicate features, making her eyes appear almost too large for her face.

Up until her suitcase had spewed her belongings over the gangway she'd looked impossibly cool and sexy in her white blouse and light cotton trousers that clung to her curvy figure. And as for those eyes! The icy look she'd given him when he'd caught her staring could have destroyed a lesser man, so the way she'd blushed when he'd retrieved her underwear had been a surprise—a good one.

She intrigued the hell out of him. Cool, almost shy one minute—and in Leith's experience women who looked like Cassie weren't in the least bit shy—sparky and determined the next.

Pity she was only here for a couple of weeks. He would have liked to take his time getting to know Dr Cassie Ross and, if she was only here for a couple of weeks, time was one thing he didn't have.

Cassie wiped the sweat from her forehead with the back of her arm and looked down at her line of patients, stretching along the dusty road and way into the distance. There wasn't room on the Mercy Ship to see outpatients, all the space being needed for the wards and theatres.

She'd seen more kids already than she could count and there were more still to be seen—most waiting patiently with their mothers, some playing in the dust and others tucked up in shawls on their mothers' backs.

It was the quiet ones you had to worry about most. Children who cried or played had to be fit enough to react to their environment. Those who lay limply in their mothers' arms were almost always the most in need of urgent attention.

On her first morning, she'd been allocated her duties by the medical officer in charge and she'd had her nose to the grindstone ever since. As the only paediatrician, Cassie was responsible for all the children the nurses referred to her at the daily morning outpatient clinic. She also had charge of the small but well-equipped children's ward and special-care facility on board and, in addition, she would assist with paediatric cases in Theatre whenever her help was required.

None of it fazed her in the slightest. She'd done a year as a surgical resident as part of her paediatric training and although didn't want to specialise in surgery had enjoyed her time in Theatre. In fact, the more challenges, the harder the work, the better.

She stopped for a moment to drink some water. In this heat it was important to keep hydrated. Suddenly, she heard a commotion in one of the other lines. Although the patients had to wait for hours in the burning sun they rarely complained so any disturbance had to mean something was wrong. With a quick word to the nurse who was assisting her, she went to see what it was about.

When she reached the point in the line where the cries had been coming from, the patients stood back. A young woman, perhaps no more than seventeen, was lying on the ground, clutching her swollen stomach and moaning with pain. Cassie dropped to her knees. Judging by the size of her abdomen, the woman was close to giving birth. Then Cassie saw something that instantly put her on red alert. There was a pool of blood soaking the woman's dress.

'Get help!' she shouted to the chattering by-standers. She instructed some of the women to form a shield and lifted the woman's dress. Her thighs were covered in blood. This was a pos-sible placental abruption—an obstetric emer-gency—and not Cassie's area of expertise. Unless the woman had a Caesarean in the next few minutes and was transfused, she would die.

As Cassie lifted her head to shout for a stretcher, someone crouched down next to her. It was the man from the gangway—Dr Ballan-tyne. Apart from that first day, four days ago, she hadn't spoken to him. She'd seen him about, of course, he wasn't exactly the kind of man that blended into his surroundings, but, as she'd promised herself, she'd gone out of her way to avoid him. Why that was she wasn't quite sure. Only that he unsettled her—and she didn't like being unsettled.

'Hello again,' he said quietly. Without Cassie having to say anything, he took in the situation at a glance. 'Looks like a possible placenta abruption,' he said grimly. 'There's no time to take her to Theatre on board. We'll have to get her inside and operate here.'

Cassie looked around. They could do with some help—a nurse and an anaesthetist for a start. But most of the doctors and nurses had stopped for lunch and retreated to the shady, cool dining room on the ship.

'We need a stretcher over here,' Leith called out. Cassie breathed a sigh of relief when two nurses emerged from the interior of one of the huts. One of the local volunteers brought a stretcher and working together they loaded the stricken woman onto it.

'I need an anaesthetist,' Leith said. 'Like now.'

'They're all on board,' the nurse said. 'Do you want me to send for one of them?'

'Yes. Go!' As soon as the nurse had taken off, Leith looked at Cassie. 'Even if she finds someone straight away, by the time they get here it will be too late. Have you ever given a spinal?'

Cassie nodded. She brought up a mental image of a medical textbook. Luckily she had an almost encyclopaedic memory, one of the few benefits of a childhood spent mostly with books.

Although she'd been warned that working on the Mercy Ship might mean stepping out of her own area of expertise, she hadn't expected to be assisting with a case of placental abruption quite so soon after her arrival. She was glad that Leith was there and appeared to be taking it all in his stride.

As he prepped the patient's abdomen, Cassie loaded a syringe with local anaesthetic. Then they turned the woman on her side and Leith held her firmly while Cassie cupped the expectant mother's hips, feeling for the bones of the pelvis. Bringing her thumbs towards the middle line and on either side of the spine, she found the space between the L3 and L4 vertebrae. She moved up to the next space. It was important to take her time. If she gave it in the wrong place, the woman could be paralysed, but in the end the spinal went every bit as smoothly as she'd anticipated.

While they waited for the anaesthetic to take effect Leith took blood for cross-matching and gave the sample to the nurse to take to the ship's laboratory. Waiting for the results would take time—when every minute could mean the difference between life and survival.

In the meantime, the midwife had returned, bringing some bags of saline back with her, and Leith immediately set about putting up a drip.

'They are preparing a theatre for you,' the midwife said.

'It's too late,' Leith replied. Cassie ignored the flutter of anxiety in her abdomen and made sure to keep her expression noncommittal. Another skill she had mastered in her childhood.

As soon as she was satisfied that the woman couldn't feel anything below her waist, she nodded to Leith, who started to operate. With Cassie keeping an eye on the woman's breathing, he sliced into the abdomen and a few minutes later pulled out a small, perfectly formed baby, who was, however, disturbingly limp and still. Cassie stepped forward and as soon as she had checked that there were no secretions blocking the airway of the baby girl, she immediately began to breathe into the newborn's mouth. *Go on, little one. Breathe for me. If not for me, for your mummy. Come on, you can do it.*

To her relief, after a few breaths the child gave a gasp and a cry. When she glanced at Leith he grinned and gave her a thumbs-up. She smiled back at him. They'd saved this baby.

They weren't out of the woods yet. The neonate needed to be taken on board the Mercy Ship and straight to the special-care nursery.

Thankfully, just at that moment another two nurses, pushing a portable incubator, rushed into the room. Now the baby would get the mechanical support she required and once she got to the ship she would have the all help the singing and dancing tiny special-care unit could give her. As the midwives transferred the baby to the incubator, Cassie glanced back at the baby's mother and was alarmed to see that blood had pooled in her abdomen.

'Damn. I'm going to have to do a hysterectomy,' Leith said. 'But she'll need to be fully anaesthetised first. That isn't something I can do here. We need to get her to Theatre.'

As Leith started to pack the pelvis with swabs, one of the other doctors hurried into the room. Knowing that she would only get in the way if she stayed, Cassie left the mother in their hands and accompanied the baby and incubator back on board.

Once the baby was settled, Cassie handed over her care to the neonatal nurse. Although the baby was slightly smaller than Cassie would have liked, she was breathing well on her own. As soon as the mother had recovered from her anaesthetic, a nurse would bring baby to her to have a feed.

By now it was after one and Cassie had to return to her clinic to see the patients still waiting, and after she'd finished there she was due in Theatre to assist with an operation. Knowing it was unlikely that she would have time for a sit-down lunch, she grabbed a sandwich from the hospital canteen before making her way on deck for a five-minute break.

She closed her eyes and let the sea breeze cool her cheeks. Immediately an image of Leith filled her head. Whenever she'd seen him on the ship, he'd been playing cards or teasing the nurses, as if medicine was the last thing on his mind. Occasionally, he'd glance her way, but she avoided his eyes and always found a seat as far away from him as possible.

Which one was the real Leith? The flirtatious, I-know-I'm-sexy-doctor of their first meeting or the one who'd been so focussed on his patient he'd barely noticed her? She shook her head. Why was she even thinking like this? She wasn't beyond having an affair, especially with someone she was unlikely to ever see again, but not with a co-worker. That, she knew, could get uncomfortable when it came to the parting of ways, which it inevitably did, as soon as they tried to turn the relationship into something it wasn't.

She took a last bite from her sandwich and chucked the remains into the bin.

No, she decided, it was better to trust her first instinct and keep well away from Dr Leith Ballantyne.

Just over five hours later Cassie was still in Theatre. The surgeon she was assisting was operating on a patient Cassie had examined at her first clinic and put forward for surgery. The teen had the biggest tumour Cassie had ever seen. Untreated, it had swollen to the size of a football, pushing the boy's features out of alignment so that his nose and mouth were grotesquely out of place. It wasn't that the benign tumour was life-threatening, but his unusual appearance had meant that he was ostracised in his village. Her heart went out to him. She knew what it felt like to feel as if you didn't fit in, and it had to be a hundred times worse for him.

Cassie stretched to ease the kinks from her back. The operation had been fascinating. The surgeon—Dr Blunt, who had worked on the Mercy Ship for the five years since she'd retired from a hospital in Boston, had told Cassie that she'd had more experience of dealing with this kind of tumour than she liked. However, she'd removed the growth with the minimum of bleeding and damage to healthy tissue.

There had been a scary moment when one of the blood vessels had started bleeding but Cassie had kept calm and managed to clamp it off without too much difficulty.

They stood back for a moment and surveyed their work. Even with the swelling, the boy looked much more normal. He'd never be a pin-up, but he wouldn't look out of place.

'Good job, Dr Ross,' Dr Blunt said. Although the operation had been a success, Cassie couldn't help but wonder if they could have made a better job of putting the boy's face back together. That was the problem. She was never satisfied. Only perfection would suffice.

She let the theatre nurse remove her gown and dropped her gloves into the bin. The thought of still having to pound the decks for her nightly run made her feel even more exhausted, but the habit was ingrained and she knew she would sleep better for it afterwards. First, though, she needed a few minutes to unwind.

She stepped out on the deck of the ship and drew in deep lungfuls of fresh air. Although the sun had dipped below the horizon, the air was still muggy and almost immediately she felt perspiration trickle down her back under her scrubs. She would wait until it was cooler to have her run and besides she wanted to check on her patient when he'd recovered from the anaesthetic.

A spurt of laughter came from below her. The staff not in Theatre or on the wards had gathered for dinner and were no doubt sharing their stories of the day. Cassie moved away, seeking the quieter starboard side—the one that faced the sea. There was a spot there behind the lifeboats where she often went when she wanted to be alone—no easy feat when there were four hundred staff on board.

To her dismay, someone had got there before her. A tall figure was leaning against one of the struts, staring out over the ocean. She was about to tiptoe away when he turned. She recognised him immediately.

He smiled at her. 'Dr Ross.' She had to admit she liked his voice with its attractive Scottish burr. 'I didn't get the chance to thank you for your help earlier today.'

'I didn't do much.' Cassie shrugged. 'How is your patient?'

'I had to do a complete hysterectomy. She won't be having any more children.'

'Perhaps that's for the best.' The area was so drought-stricken that despite everything the Mercy Ship and aid workers were doing, too many children were dying from starvation and, with clean water still a scarce resource, disease.

Leith looked at her in surprise. 'I doubt she'll see it that way.'

'At least she has a living child. I saw the baby earlier and she's going to be fine. Surely it is better for a mother to have one healthy child than several sick children?'

'I don't think we can apply our Western standards here, at least not without understanding more about the culture.'

Feeling as if she was being lectured, Cassie bristled. But before she could respond he went on.

'I watched you while you were assisting in Theatre earlier. You have deft hands.'

She hadn't noticed him among the observers in the gallery.

'Thank you—er—Dr Ballantyne. '

Amusement glinted in his jade-green eyes. 'How very formal. Call me Leith.'

'Very well. Thank you, Leith.' God, she sounded as if she was an awkward teen being introduced to her first boy. 'If you'll excuse me, I have to go and check on my patient.' She didn't really want to get into a conversation. Quite the opposite. For some reason she wanted to run away from this man as fast as she could.

He looked into her eyes for a second longer than was strictly professional before giving her a grin that sent her heart spinning.

* * *

Most days, as soon as she'd finished her early morning ward rounds, Cassie would make her way on shore and over to the school. Since their brief encounter on deck, Cassie found herself searching more often than she cared to admit for glimpses of Leith, but although they'd exchanged nods and smiles of greeting, to her relief—at least she told herself it was relief—he hadn't sought her out.

As often happened, the sun was beginning to set by the time the last patient had been seen. Cassie was taking a few moments to admire the reddening sky when she sensed, rather than saw, Leith come to stand next to her. To her dismay, her heart rate went into overdrive.

'Finished for the day?' he asked with a smile. His white, short-sleeved cotton shirt emphasised the dark hairs on his chest and his muscular forearms. Why on earth was she even noticing?

'Yes. Apart from ward rounds before bed.' Cassie turned her face upwards, enjoying the feel of the early evening breeze on her overheated skin. 'What about you?'

He rubbed his stubbly chin. 'Me too.' They

stood together in silence as the sun flared, turning the soil pink.

'Such a beautiful country,' Cassie said softly, 'despite its problems.'

When he looked at her, her pulse upped yet another notch. His eyes were the colour of summer grass, she thought distractedly. She gave herself a mental shake and glanced away. What was wrong with her, for heaven's sake? Never before had she felt such instant attraction and it scared her.

Just then she noticed that a woman from the village was standing a couple of feet away, waiting patiently.

'Doctor—come with me. Please?' she said.

'What is it?' Leith asked. 'Is someone in trouble?'

The woman glanced around anxiously. 'Please. Just come. You both.'

Leith raised an eyebrow at Cassie. 'Are you up for it?'

It was as if every nerve in her body was screeching at her to run—to keep her distance from this man. Which was ridiculous. Someone needed their help and of course she wouldn't—couldn't—say no.

When she nodded the woman smiled with relief. 'My name is Precious,' she said. 'It is my sister, Maria, I want you to see.'

They followed Precious in the failing light along a narrow track. The cicadas had started chirping and the sounds of Africa permeated the night air. As the path entered a small stretch of trees the sun disappeared completely. Soon it was too dark to see properly, although the woman leading the way appeared to have no difficulty. Cassie stumbled over the root of a tree and Leith caught her hand. A spark shot up her arm and she had to resist the urge to pull away.

Still holding her hand and close on the heels of Precious, he guided Cassie along the path, pointing out intruding thorns from acacia trees and other obstacles for her to avoid.

A short while later they came to a cluster of huts. The villagers, lit only by the glow of the evening meal fires, were making preparations for the night.

But instead of stopping at one of the huts, the woman led them through the village and back into the darkness. Cassie had a moment's doubt. This was a poor country and it was possible that the woman was leading them into a trap. But they couldn't turn away now.

The thought clearly hadn't crossed Leith's mind as his footsteps never faltered. About two kilometres further on, with the village left far behind them, the woman stopped. At first Cassie could see nothing but then, as the woman pointed, she could make out a small hut in the shadows. This was unexpected. The villagers lived in close proximity to one another. Who could be living so far away from the comfort and help of others?

Precious led them inside. A young woman was crouched over a small fire, mixing a pot of mielie meal with a stick while a small child, no more than two, sat on the bed, watching her.

'This is Maria,' Precious said, before turning back to the woman and speaking rapidly in the vernacular.

Cassie couldn't understand a word but it sounded reassuring. When Precious had finished talking, the mother looked at them with a mixture of hope and despair.

'Maria has been sent away from the village.' Precious said.

'Why?' Cassie asked.

When Precious hesitated, Leith's brow knotted. 'I suspect I know the reason.' He turned to their guide. 'Has Maria been wetting herself?

'Will she allow me to examine her?' Leith asked.

Precious translated and, blushing deeply, Maria lay down on top of the bed after lifting the child and placing him on a rush mat. He stared silently with big, brown eyes.

'I will go and fetch some water,' Precious said, and slipped outside.

In the silence the little boy continued to watch them. Then he slid off the mat and toddled over to Cassie, lifting his hands. Instinctively Cassie reached down and picked him up. The child snuggled into her, peeping out at his mother.

'Seems he's taken a liking to you,' Leith said with a smile.

'Children seem to like me—which is an advantage given my line of work,' she responded lightly. Without warning an image flashed into her head. She couldn't have been very much older than this child—perhaps three or four. She'd fallen over and scraped her knee and had gone crying to her mother and held up her hands, wanting to be lifted, to have her hurt made better.

To her bewilderment her mother had turned away, saying it was only a scrape and not to make a fuss. But before she'd turned away, Cassie had seen something in her eyes that had made her forget about the pain in her knee and feel pain in her chest instead. Later she'd come to realise it had been dislike she'd seen.

When the time had come to choose which medical speciality to pursue, she'd been drawn to paediatrics. Perhaps because she wanted to rescue all the little Cassies out there. But she would never risk becoming a mother herself— experience had taught her that too often the worst parents were those who had been badly, or inadequately, parented themselves. Nevertheless, just because she wasn't going to have children herself, it didn't mean she didn't love having them as her patients.

'Cassie? You okay?' Leith's voice pulled her back to the present. She forced a smile and tightened her hold on the little boy in her arms. 'Sure. A little hot—that's all.'

Looking puzzled, Leith continued to hold her gaze, but when she returned his stare steadily he gave his head a little shake and focussed his attention back on Maria.

Leith examined the woman discreetly and gently, before straightening. 'As I thought, she has a fistula from her bowel into her vagina, which has led to her being incontinent. I've treated a few women with this condition since I've been here. They tend to be ostracised by their fellow villagers and rarely come for help, although I suspect that finally word is getting around that we can often do something for them.'

'Poor thing,' Cassie said. 'And can you? Help her?'

He smiled. 'Yes, I'm confident I can fix her problem.' He turned to Precious. 'She must come to the hospital ship. Tomorrow. Tell her I will have to operate, but it is a simple procedure and after she will be much better.'

Precious broke into a wide smile. 'She will be so happy. It has been hard for her here, all alone with her child. I can only help a little—I have my own family to care for.' She turned to her sister and spoke rapidly. With tears in her eyes, Maria reached out for Cassie's hand and said something Cassie couldn't understand.

'She asks if you will be there. She says you have a kind face. Like the other doctor.' Precious glanced at Leith and smiled shyly. 'But she will feel better if there is another woman.'

Cassie thought rapidly. She had a full clinic in the morning and was scheduled to assist with a couple of operations before then. Then she looked at the small child and the mother and knew that, whatever it took, she would find a way to be present. How could she deny Maria this one small thing?

Precious led them back to the village but once there Leith assured her that he and Cassie would find their own way back to the ship. Cassie wasn't so sure. The night was dark beyond the village and without so much as a torch to light their way it would be difficult to find the path. But as Precious clearly wanted to return to her sister, Cassie swallowed her anxiety and followed Leith. As he strode confidently into the bush, it seemed as if he had no problem seeing in the dark.

She kept her eyes on his broad back, pausing when he did and stepping over the roots of trees that he pointed out. They must have been almost halfway back to where the ship was docked when suddenly Leith stood stock still as if listening for something. Then he let out a yell and hit something from the back of his neck. It fell to the ground and Cassie heard the rustle of leaves as it scuttled away.

'God! What the hell was that?' Leith said, his face pale in the light of the moon.

'A bird or a spider, I suspect,' she said, trying not to laugh.

'If it was a spider it must have been a bloody huge one.'

'Whatever it was, it's gone. You're safe now. I promise I won't let that horrible beastie get you.'

He must have heard the amusement in her voice as he looked sheepish. 'Not very macho, was it? Jumping four feet in the air.' He grinned, his teeth flashing whitely in the dark. 'Spiders and I don't go together very well.'

Cassie smiled back. 'Don't worry, your secret is safe with me. I won't tell anyone.' And then, just like that, she knew that whatever she'd been telling herself about staying away from this man, it was too late.

CHAPTER TWO

AS SHE PROMISED, the next day Cassie joined Leith in Theatre once her own session had finished. His patient hadn't been put under yet so Cassie went over to her and squeezed her hand. Maria smiled tremulously.

'It's going to be okay,' Cassie whispered, knowing that the woman probably couldn't understand her but hoping she found her tone reassuring.

She stood back while Leith repaired the tear, which, judging by the image on the monitor, was significant. Happily, the Mercy Ship had many generous donors and was equipped with the best and latest high-tech equipment.

'She must have torn during labour—I'm pretty sure it must have been a breech delivery, 'Leith said as he worked. 'She's probably lucky to have survived. I'm guessing there was a great deal of bleeding.'

Cassie admired his surgical technique. He wasted no time and his stitching was neat. As he operated he explained to the nurses what he was doing. When he'd finished he looked up with a satisfied smile. 'I don't think she'll have any more problems.' He peeled off his gloves and chucked them in the bin. 'She'll need to stay in for a few days.'

Cassie walked with him to the door, glancing at her watch. She had thirty minutes—just enough time for a quick shower and change of scrubs before she was due at her outpatient clinic.

'Meet me later?' Leith asked quietly.

Cassie's heart thumped. She already knew she wasn't going to say no. Last night she'd tossed and turned, thinking about Leith and wondering what she would do if he sought her out. She'd managed to convince herself that it could do no harm to spend time with him. She was tired of her own company and Leith was, well, interesting to say the least. It wasn't as if there was any danger of them having more than a short while together. Pretty soon they'd be going their separate ways.

'Why not? Let's meet at the harbour wall. Say, around seven-thirty?'

Leith grinned and her heart did a little somer-sault. Good God, it was like being a teenager again, except no one had ever made her feel like this. Not as a teenager, not as an adult, not ever. Determined to ignore the warning bells in her head, she gave him one last smile and headed to the changing rooms.

Over the next week they spent almost all their off-duty hours together and Cassie found herself constantly looking out for him as she worked. She was happy—yet terrified. In the past, when-ever she had found herself getting too close to a man, she'd simply backed away before the rela-tionship had got too serious, and every day she told herself to walk away from Leith while she could.

But her resolve melted away as soon as she saw him. Why not enjoy what they had while she could? It wasn't as if Leith made demands on her, simply seeming to enjoy her company, although she suspected, from the way he looked at her, that he wasn't immune either.

Was it possible that finally she'd met someone she could love and, even more importantly, who could love her in return? She groaned inwardly. What was the use in even thinking like that? She had her future all mapped out and it didn't—couldn't—include long-term relationships.

'Where will you go when you're finished here?' Leith asked one evening as they walked along the beach.

'I have a job with the United Nations—in their International Medical Corps.'

He whistled. 'The United Nations! A high-flyer, then?'

She smiled up at him. 'That's one way of putting it.' She had certainly worked hard enough to achieve her dreams. Always refusing to go out with her fellow medical students, although that hadn't simply been down to work, being the first on the wards and last off as a trainee, doing anything and everything that had been asked of her. After all, she of all people knew how to please.

But she didn't want to think about that. It was the present she cared about right now. 'My first posting is to Sudan. I go straight there from here.'

He frowned. 'Why Sudan?'

'I can't think of a more worthwhile use of my skills. I like the feeling I'm helping children in real need.' She breathed in the scent of sea and spice that she'd come to associate with Africa. 'And I've always wanted to travel,' she added. *Because no place felt like home.* 'I think it will be a real test of my skills. What about you?'

'I worked as a consultant in Glasgow for years and spent a long time abroad—mainly Africa but other countries too. I moved to London a couple of years ago. I work in Harley Street now.'

'Harley Street?' Cassie said, surprised. 'Bit of a shift from Africa to Harley Street, isn't it?'

'Hey, don't mock what you don't know. The practice I work for only employs the best—its patients won't tolerate anything else.' He grinned at her. 'If you're ever looking for a job, I know they'd like to have a top-class doctor on the team.'

Warmth spread through her at the compliment. Although she knew she was a good doctor, she wasn't used to praise. It felt good, especially so, she had to admit, coming from Leith. But of course what he was suggesting was impossible.

'Thanks, but, no, thanks. London in the rain? The crowds? Battling the Underground? Give me blue skies and sun any time,' she responded, knowing it was only a version of the truth. 'I've had my career all mapped out ever since I went into medicine. That's the way I like my life. It keeps me focussed.'

'What about the personal one?'

The look in his eyes made her bones melt and once again she found herself wondering if there could be room in her life for spontaneity. Did everything have to be planned down to the last hour? On the other hand, that *was* how she liked it. It was far safer.

'My work gives me everything I need—or want.'

He raised his eyebrow. 'Everything? You don't intend to get married? Have children?'

She stiffened. 'Not every woman is born to be a mother.'

'No,' he replied, looking surprised, 'but I've seen the way you are with the children. You're a natural.'

'Why does everyone think that every woman should want to have a child? In my experience, some women should be positively banned from having kids. After all, no one seems to think it unnatural if a man doesn't want to have children. What about you, for example? Are they in your future?'

'One day perhaps.' His eyes crinkled at the corners. 'In a few years' time. In the meantime, I plan to have as much fun as I can.'

Her heart sank. His reply wasn't what she'd wanted to hear.

'And your parents? Are they in London?' he continued after a moment's silence.

Suddenly chilled, despite the muggy evening, she wrapped her arms around herself. 'Some of the time. They spend a lot of time abroad now. One way or another, I don't see much of them. What about yours?' She wasn't about to tell him that a bonus of going to work in Sudan was its distance from her adoptive parents.

He studied her for a moment as if he was about to press her further but then he seemed to change his mind. 'They live on Skye. They've been married for forty years and still crazily in love with each other. That's the way I want it to be if ever I get married.'

A familiar ache in her chest made her catch her breath. Wouldn't it be wonderful to believe love could last? They halted under an acacia tree. In the distance, small fishing boats lit by glowing lanterns bobbed about the waters of the Atlantic Ocean and the smell of jasmine hung on the heavy night air.

Leith tipped her chin so she was looking up at him. 'God, you're beautiful.' The world stopped turning as he brought his mouth down on hers. For a moment she felt as if she could hardly breathe. His kiss was gentle at first, his lips warm and questioning. But as she melted into him, his kiss became deeper, more demanding, and she wrapped her arms around his neck, wanting more of him.

She could feel his desire for her against her pelvis and an answering warmth flooded through her. She wanted him. She wanted to feel his naked skin on hers, to have his hands all over her body and hers on his. She didn't even care that after she'd left here she would never see him again—all she needed right now was this.

When they pulled away they were both breathing deeply.

'Come back to the ship with me,' he said simply.

When she nodded, he took her hand.

Cassie woke to bright sunshine streaming in through the porthole. At first she didn't know where she was, but as the fog of sleep lifted she remembered. She smiled and stretched as a warm peace filled her. She couldn't remember the last time she felt this good.

She propped herself up on her elbow and studied Leith. Even in his sleep his mouth turned up at the corners. She trailed her fingertips over the hard contours of his chest and as she did so his eyes snapped open and he caught her hand in his.

'Morning,' he said with a smile.

'Morning,' she whispered back.

He ran his hand along her shoulder and down the curve of her waist and every nerve in her body tingled. They had made love twice last night, but now she wanted him again with a need that shocked her.

She moulded the length of her body against

his so that it seemed as if every inch of her skin was in contact with his.

He pulled her tighter. 'I can't seem to get enough of you,' he groaned.

Or her him. They didn't have long, but why think about the future and what couldn't be? Why not just be happy while she could?

It was her last coherent thought before she gave herself up to him.

Leith found himself humming under his breath at the oddest moments and when he wasn't with Cassie he was thinking about her. He constantly sought her out and loved to catch even the briefest glimpses of her, squatting on her heels in the dust, talking to a group of women, or distracting a child while carrying out some unpleasant procedure by making funny faces or dangling a colourful toy just out of reach before relinquishing it to them.

Sometimes he would find her on her own on the deck of the ship, staring out to sea with a wistful, almost sad expression on her face. But then she would catch sight of him and her face would be transformed by the smile he'd grown to love. It felt as if their coming together had been inevitable. Which was strange—very strange. He wasn't a man who believed in fate.

However, it felt good. It felt right.

But he still knew little more about her than he'd known at the start. Normally that would be good but with Cassie he wanted to know it all. In the past he'd always kept his relationships light-hearted and stayed away from the heavy stuff, but no one had made him feel the way he had since the first moment he'd spotted her lugging her suitcase along the quay.

However, he wasn't going to think about what might or might not be. He was going to make the most of being with Cassie while he could.

He was smiling as he opened the email he'd received that morning.

He read it through and clicked on the attachment. It was a photograph of a boy of around four with large green eyes. He stared disbelievingly at an image that could have been him as a child.

An hour later, Leith was still trying to come to terms with what he'd learned. He had a son. He was a father. It just didn't compute. Okay, so he'd always thought that he might, one day, have children, but 'one day' were the two key words. One day in the future. So far in the future he couldn't even really imagine it.

But he'd better start imagining it.

He had a child.

He wasn't ready to be a father. Not yet. He liked his life just the way it was. No ties, no obligations. Doing what he wanted. Work, women and travel—that's what he liked. A child would put a stop to that. He'd have to be responsible, for God's sake. Cut down on his working hours, reduce his travel commitments, be selective about the women he dated.

He examined the picture for the umpteenth time. The child was clearly bright—anyone could see that. And he had the same set to his jaw that Leith recognised from his own childhood pictures, which his mother brought out every time he was at home; hundreds of him as a baby naked on a blanket, as a toddler standing proudly next to his father with his own child-sized fishing rod, on his mother's lap as she read him a story, all depicting the years until his graduation photograph and beyond. As his racing mind conjured up an image of him taking his son fishing or out on the boat, just as his father had taken him, something shifted inside his chest.

He studied the photograph again. In his childhood photographs he was always smiling—he might look the worse for wear, with patches on his knees and a dirt-smeared face, but he always looked blissfully happy.

He drew closer to the screen and his skin chilled. His son didn't look happy—he didn't look happy at all.

No child of his should look like that.

Cassie was happier than she could ever remember being. After the night she'd spent with Leith, they took every moment they could to be together. As soon as their medical duties were over they'd slip away, either to walk into the African veld or sometimes take a blanket down to the beach where they'd sit and talk about their day as the waves lapped against the shore.

Her heart cracked a little every time she thought about it ending. Leaving wasn't supposed to be this hard. Wasn't this the reason she'd always promised herself never to care too much?

Tonight they were sitting on their favourite spot by the shore. Leith was behind her with his legs and arms wrapped around her as she rested against his chest.

'Do you have to go to Sudan?' he asked suddenly.

The question caught her unawares and silence hung heavily before she answered. 'Why? What else would you have me do?' she asked lightly.

'Come to London. You could get a job with the practice or in one of the teaching hospitals. Someone with your credentials should find it easy to get a job anywhere.'

She doodled a picture in the sand, stalling for time. 'Now, why should I do that?'

His arms tightened around her. 'I'm not ready to let you go.'

Her breath stopped in her throat. For a moment her carefully constructed future held no allure, her need and want of him overriding every rational thought. Perhaps it needn't end? The thought shook her. Was she really thinking that this could last? What he was asking was impossible—she couldn't let her employers down at this late stage. Especially not for a dream that might not come to anything. 'I can't not go to Sudan, Leith. I've made a commitment.'

She felt his sigh. 'Damn it.'

Wriggling out of his arms, she turned to face him.

'You could come with me. They're always looking for people.'

'I can't.' His voice was flat, his expression unreadable.

The light inside her flickered and died. She had read too much into his words. He wanted her to come to him but he wasn't prepared to do the same for her.

'But we could meet again when you to return to London,' he added. 'Until then, we could write, email, phone even. I'm sure they have phones in Sudan.' His eyes glittered in the moonlight as he searched her face. She could almost hear the thudding of her own heart.

Why not? Perhaps it was time she trusted her heart to someone. To Leith. Take a chance. The thought was hammering around inside her head. Go on, take a chance. This man could love you—really love you.

But would he love her for ever? Could love ever be for ever? Could fairy-tales come true?

She leaned towards him and pulled his head towards hers. 'Enough of the talking,' she said lightly. 'Do you know it's been at least twenty minutes since you last kissed me?'

All too soon it was their last night together. The boat was setting sail at dawn to go further up the coast and it would be leaving her behind to catch her flight to Sudan. Leith still had a few days left before he too would be returning to his job in London.

Sometimes Cassie fantasised about the life they could have together but deep down she knew it was only that—a fantasy. Despite the passion they had for one another's bodies, they hardly knew each other. She had her life to lead, one that didn't include children—or a permanent relationship.

But there were still a few hours left for them to be together and she was determined to make the most of every second.

She was lying in the crook of Leith's arm as one of his hands brushed lazily along her shoulder. Over the last couple of days he'd seemed preoccupied. She'd often catch him looking into the distance as if he were miles away, but she didn't ask. If he had something to tell her, let it be in his own time. She hated people's questions too much to ever pry.

But tonight he seemed particularly distracted. Normally when they were together he focussed his full attention on her. She'd noticed that he did the same whatever he was doing, working, eating—or making love. At the memory of just how thoroughly he'd made love to her only moments before, her whole body tingled. She stretched languorously.

'Penny for them,' she said, wondering if he was thinking about a patient.

'I'm not sure you'd want to hear them.'

A shiver ran down her spine. There was something ominous about the tone of his voice.

'As long as you're not going to tell me you're married after all.' She laughed nervously.

His hand stilled on her shoulder. 'No,' he said.

'Of course it's not that.' He paused for a moment. 'I had an email a couple of days ago.'

She propped herself onto her elbow and looked down at him. Anxiety fluttered when she saw he was frowning. 'Bad news?'

'No. Yes. Damn it. I don't know. A bit of both.' He swung his legs out of bed and pulled on his jeans. The only light came from the moon shining through the open curtains. Even in the half-light, he was unbelievably gorgeous with his hair tousled by their lovemaking, his skin golden from the African sun and his broad shoulders that tapered to slim hips and long legs. When he turned his intense green eyes on her, her heart lurched at the thought that soon she would lose him.

Since the night he'd suggested they keep in touch, he'd been strangely silent on the subject. Had he changed his mind? Or had she simply read more into his words than he'd meant? Had it been no more than a casual throw-away comment and was this the part when he told her it had been great but…?

She plucked nervously at the trimming of the sheets.

'I'm afraid you're going to have to explain.'

He sank down on the bed and pulled her against his bare chest. She lay there for a moment, listening to the beating of his heart.

'I had a one-night stand a few years ago,' he said finally. 'Until recently I had forgotten about it.'

Cassie stiffened in his arms. She shouldn't be surprised he had a past.

'Her name was Jude. To be honest, I barely even remembered that. Anyway, her sister, Bella, wrote to me. It seems Jude had a child—about nine months after we had our—er—thing.'

A chill ran up Cassie's spine. 'You didn't take precautions?'

He rubbed his hand across the rough stubble of his face. 'It had been a tough day. She told me she was on the Pill. I chose to believe her.'

Cassie guessed what was coming next. 'She had your baby.'

'Apparently,' he said dryly.

'She didn't tell you? So why has the sister written now?' The hollow feeling in her stomach was getting worse. She wriggled out of his arms.

'Because she's worried. Bella's been trying to

persuade Jude to tell me that I have a son ever since Jude told her she was pregnant, but she wouldn't.'

'So what's changed now?'

'Bella doesn't think Jude is coping with him. She's even hinted that Jude's been taking drugs.' He raked his hand through his hair. 'God, Cassie, what kind of mother would do that when she has a small child to take care of?'

Cassie hugged her knees to her chest. She knew only too well what kind of woman. Someone like her own birth mother for a start.

She felt horribly disappointed. Had she misjudged him completely? Had she been too quick to put him on a pedestal? Of course it was ridiculous to think anyone was without flaws—she of all people should know that.

'I'm pretty sure she wasn't on any drugs when we met. According to the family her drug taking only started a couple of years ago. And as to why she should feel it necessary not to tell me she was expecting our child, Lord knows, I haven't all the details yet. Possibly because there was a man in her life, someone she was engaged to, when she and I had our—er—thing, and before you say anything I swear I didn't know. Anyway, he left her when he found out the baby wasn't his. Apparently that's when Jude started behaving erratically.'

Poor Jude. But it was the little boy that Cassie's heart went out to. Why did people have children if they weren't capable of looking after them? When she felt all the old anger boil up inside her, she pushed it away before it could take hold.

'Although he's only four, Jude's sister thinks that the boy is being badly affected by his mother's behaviour.' Leith rose from their narrow bed and started pacing up and down the small cabin.

'What are you going to do?'

'If he's my child, and I have no doubt he is judging by the photo the sister emailed me, then I'm going to do whatever it takes to get access to him—fight for sole custody even if need be.'

He strode over to his laptop and flipped the lid. He typed something into the browser and turned the monitor so Cassie could see. 'The sister sent me this picture of him.'

Cassie wrapped herself in a sheet and went to stand next to Leith. Immediately, just by looking at the little boy's eyes, Cassie knew without doubt he was Leith's son. The circumference of Leith's iris was slightly irregular—barely noticeable unless, like Cassie, a person had spent a lot of time looking into his green eyes. This little boy had exactly the same irregularity in the same eye. But it wasn't just the family resemblance that drew Cassie. In the child's eyes she recognised the same bewilderment and pain that she'd seen in the rare photos of herself at the same age. She sucked in a breath, conscious of a knot in her stomach. An image rushed back of her as a little girl, having woken from a bad dream, sitting on the top of the stairs, praying that her mum would come and carry her back to bed, kiss her, say or do anything to make the ghosts and demons of the night go away. But when Mum hadn't answered her calls, she had got cold and had eventually crept back to bed alone and miserable.

'What's his name?' she asked, swallowing hard.

'Peter.'

'Where do they live?'

'In Bristol.'

'So what next?'

Leith raked a hand through his hair again and stared back at the computer screen, his expression bleak. 'As soon as I get back to London, I'm going to consult a lawyer. If necessary, I'll have him removed from his mother's care.'

'Perhaps you should meet Peter and his mother first? Talk to her. Maybe there will be no need for lawyers. If you involve them now, it's possible Peter will be taken into care while access is sorted. Is that what you want? Think of him. Sometimes any sort of mother—if she loves the child—is better than a substitute.'

Leith narrowed his eyes. 'I want my son. And if Jude isn't able to look after him, then I want him away from her.'

This steel was a side to the normally easygoing Leith she hadn't seen before. Chilled, she went back to bed and huddled under the thin duvet.

Leith's pager buzzed. He cursed as he looked at the message that had come up. 'There's an emergency in Theatre and they need my help. Can we talk about this later?'

'I'm leaving before the ship sails,' she reminded him.

'I'll be back as soon as I can.' He tugged on his

shirt. 'Damn the timing. I haven't even got your address or phone number,' he groaned, tossing his mobile to her. 'Could you put it in for me?' He glanced at his watch, hopping on one foot as he pulled his left shoe on. 'But be sure to come and find me if I get held up.' Then he gathered her against him and kissed her hungrily.

Despite everything, Cassie melted into him and responded with a passion that, until she'd met Leith, she hadn't known she was capable of.

He released her reluctantly. 'God, I would give anything to be back in bed with you, woman, but I have to go. I'll see you later.' And with that he was gone.

For a long time after Leith had left Cassie lay on the bed, wrestling with her thoughts.

Leith had a child and that changed everything.

When she'd agreed to keep in touch that had been before…before she'd known he had a child.

She couldn't be with Leith if he had a child. Particularly one who was bound to be needy. The parallels between her life and Peter's were uncanny and she couldn't, just couldn't, risk becoming even slightly involved in the life of a vulnerable child and riding the emotional roller-coaster along with him and his father.

But, a little voice whispered, *it's not as if he's asking you to be a mother to his child.*

It didn't matter if he was asking or not. He wasn't the kind of man who would put his child aside for anyone. If he had been, she couldn't love him the way she did.

And she did. Love him. With all her heart and soul, and would for the rest of her days.

But be a mother to his child? If it ever came to that?

No.

She didn't know how.

She wasn't up to the task. She couldn't be objective enough, and soon, in all likelihood, she and Leith would end up disagreeing about what was best for Peter and he would be caught in the middle, her own objectivity compromised by a lifetime of hurt. Of course it was impossible.

She couldn't be with Leith. Her throat closed. All her dreams of a fairy-tale ending had been just that—a dream.

Flinging back the covers, Cassie dragged herself out of bed and started getting dressed. There was still the rest of her packing and a thousand other things to do and she didn't want to be here when he returned. Better to end it now, quickly and as pain-free as possible. Leith and his son deserved better. They deserved someone who could be part of their family, not a damaged woman who had no intention of being a mother—not even a stepmother—*particularly* not a stepmother. If she couldn't risk not loving a child of her own enough, how could she risk not loving Leith's son? And Leith would demand it. If she were in his shoes, she would feel the same.

As for Peter... The little boy had enough to cope with without a new woman in his father's life—one who might be there one minute and gone the next.

She tasted the salt of her tears. She loved Leith too much to get in the way of a life with his son. He would forget about her soon enough. But just in case she had to make sure he wouldn't come after her.

The tightness in her chest hurt.

She scrawled a few lines on a piece of paper she found next to his computer. Then she opened the door and slipped outside.

CHAPTER THREE

Eighteen months later

LEITH FLICKED THROUGH the CV of the applicant he and Rose were going to interview in a few minutes' time. He should have looked over it sooner, but his colleague had been particularly excited about this candidate, listing her credentials and experience, almost gloating about the number of heartfelt letters of commendation, and he hadn't felt the need to study the application until now. But he should have. Damn it, he should have. It had to be her. How many Cassie Rosses could there be who were paediatricians and who had worked on the Mercy Ship?

Only one.

Resisting the temptation to screw her CV into a ball and drop it in the wastepaper basket, he flung the application on his desk.

Why had she applied for the temporary position? She must know it was where he worked. He clearly remembered telling her he was a partner in a Harley Street practice.

But there were hundreds of practices on Harley Street and he couldn't remember if he'd actually told her which one he was a partner of. On the other hand, if she'd done her homework, she'd have seen his name listed as one of the partners.

What was she up to?

Eighteen months since he'd last seen her and she still haunted him.

She'd left without coming to find him, leaving only a note. That was all their relationship had meant to her.

That last night, the ship had sailed by the time he'd returned to his cabin. What had seemed to be a straightforward obstetric emergency had gone badly wrong when they hadn't been able to stop the woman bleeding. It had taken hours before he'd been happy to leave the labour ward. He'd known he wouldn't find Cassie, but to discover that she hadn't left her number in his phone—only a short note—had floored him. They hadn't made firm plans for the future, apart from agreeing to keep in touch, but he'd been so certain that she'd felt the same as he had that he'd imagined that one day they'd be together.

So much for his usually reliable radar when it came to women—although he would have bet his life back then that she had fallen for him as hard as he'd fallen for her.

So you got her wrong. Move on. You have enough on your plate with Peter. Let it go. Tell Rose and the others that you worked with her and you don't think she's up to it.

But he couldn't bring himself to lie. Whatever else she was, she had been a fine doctor.

And he was over her. Way over her.

He picked up the application form again. She'd spent six months in Sudan before taking a posting in Afghanistan. That had ended three months ago. What had she been doing since then?

An extended holiday? Marriage? Time off to have a child?

His stomach knotted.

What did it matter? He and Cassie Ross were history.

And the practice needed an experienced locum

to stand in for Fabio. It was only for a couple of months. Eight weeks. Possibly less.

So what harm could it do to interview her? At the very least he could finally prove to himself she meant nothing to him now.

The nightmare woke her from sleep as it had for the last three months.

Her heart still pounding, Cassie tossed the covers aside and slipped out of bed. Today of all days she had to keep it together. Crossing to the window, she threw open the curtains, wincing as bright sunlight flooded into the room. The mini heat wave that had hit London showed no signs of abating.

She showered quickly and dressed. Wiping the condensation from the bathroom mirror, she studied her reflection and sighed. She barely recognised the pale face with the dull eyes that stared back at her.

After applying foundation and blusher, she thought she looked better. She wouldn't be winning any beauty competitions in the near future, but she looked passable—professional at least.

Today she'd be seeing Leith again. Her heart

thumped painfully against her chest. Would he be married? Eighteen months was a long time and someone like Leith could never live like a monk. And as for his son, had he gained access to him?

Her hands were trembling as she applied her mascara. Was she out of her mind applying for a job at the practice where he was a partner? But what other choice did she have? Any more time cooped up in this flat on her own and she'd surely go crazy—if she wasn't already.

Stepping into the small sitting room, she glanced around. Most of what had once belonged to her beloved Nanny had been packed and donated to charity shops. The flat was bare, except for the few items of furniture Cassie couldn't bear to part with—and Martha's necklace, the one Cassie remembered her former nanny always wearing. She picked up the string of pearls, turning the cool gems between her fingers, and felt herself relax. She slipped it on and fastened it at the back.

'Wish me luck, Martha,' she whispered. 'I'm going to need it.'

* * *

The room felt as if it were closing in on Cassie. She tried to look composed, although it was almost impossible with Leith sitting opposite her and studying her through narrow, speculative eyes. She fingered the necklace around her neck for courage.

Although it had not been much more than a year and a half since she'd last seen Leith, it felt much longer. So much had happened. Physically he hadn't changed, but dressed as he was in a dark grey suit, white shirt and maroon tie, his formal appearance and cool greeting made him seem virtually a stranger to her.

No doubt he was curious as to what had brought her to apply for a job here. When she'd seen the advert in a medical journal she'd immediately wondered if it was his practice. So she'd done an internet search and, sure enough, his name had appeared as one of the partners. She'd hesitated but after waking to yet another day filled with nothing but emptiness she'd plucked up the courage to apply. Just because Leith worked there it didn't mean she couldn't apply for the temporary position they were advertising. Whatever had been between them was in the past.

But to her dismay the connection was still there—at least on her side. The air seemed to pulse between them, her body on red alert. With him so close it was impossible to suppress the images that flashed into her head; the two of them down by the shore or arms and legs entwined as they lay in bed together. She closed her eyes to shut them out. Damn.

'Are you all right?' Rose asked. 'Would you like some water?'

She needed to get a grip. She forced herself to focus on the kindly face of Rose Cavendish, the practice manager, sitting across from her. She twisted her hands together to stop them trembling and shook her head. 'No, thank you.'

Leith turned to Rose. 'Dr Ross and I worked together briefly some time ago.'

Rose's eyes widened. 'You didn't mention you'd met Cassie before.'

'Yup. Should have read the application sooner. But no matter, her referees confirmed my own impressions. No one can question her competency.' His lip curled slightly as cool green eyes swept over her.

Oh, God! He hadn't known. If he had, would she have been invited for an interview? Somehow she suspected not. Dismay washed over her. This was going from bad to worse.

'The Dr Ross I remember was about to take up a position with the United Nations,' he continued, holding her gaze. 'But I see from your CV that you stopped working with them—what, three months ago?'

Cassie chewed her lip. She'd been dreading this question.

She forced a smile. 'I had to come back to London for a while. This job was advertised as being for up to two months, which suits my current plans.' She hoped they didn't notice that she hadn't really answered their question. She didn't want to tell them that she'd spent the time in hospital, then recuperating while trying to decide what to do with the rest of her life.

Leith looked doubtful, as well he might. When she'd known him she'd been so insistent that her future was planned down to the last T. Well, let him speculate. Although there had been other jobs she could have applied for, they were either outside London or permanent posts and until she decided whether or not to return to her post with the UN, she needed to get back to work. Any more time with nothing to do but think and she'd go crazy.

'If we take you on we will want you to see the children who come to the practice,' Rose continued. 'At the moment Dr Lineham—Fabio—sees most of them but his wife is expecting and he's hoping to take some time off to be with her and the baby so you'd have sole responsibility for all our younger patients. How does that sound?'

'Perfect.'

'And you will be content to work in what essentially is a general practice?' Leith said, still looking puzzled. 'Apart from one or two of the children who have chronic or complex conditions—and Dr Lineham will still follow them up—you'll mainly be seeing the children of over-anxious parents with not much wrong with them.'

It seemed that he wasn't going to be satisfied with anything other than a full explanation. And could she blame him? She'd be asking the same questions if she were in his shoes. He wasn't to know how much she hated talking about the reasons she'd left her post with the United Nations. Everything they needed to know about her was all there in her CV.

Except it wasn't. Not everything. Not the stuff that kept her from sleeping at night.

'As I said, I need to be in London for a few months and your practice has a great reputation.'

Despite her racing heart, she held Leith's steady gaze. He was bound to question her motives for applying for this job, either suspecting her of exploiting their past relationship in order to secure a position in the well-respected, lucrative practice or—her colour deepened—to see him again. Neither could be further from the truth.

It was just one of those unfortunate coincidences that the only job on offer within the particular timeframe she wanted was this one, and she desperately, *desperately*, needed it. So it didn't matter what the hell he thought. He'd find out soon enough that she had no intention of picking up where they'd left off.

If only he would stop looking at her the way

she remembered so well—his emerald-green eyes unreadable and searching at the same time. It still felt as if he could see into her head.

Judging by Leith's frown, he wanted a better explanation than the one she'd given. Just in time she stopped herself from rubbing the scar on the inside of her arm.

'My friend died recently and left me her London flat. I need time to sort it out before I put it on the market.' How easily the words slipped out. Nanny *had* been a friend—more than a friend. She'd given her the only consistent mothering Cassie had ever known, and the flat she'd left her the only place that had felt like home. Her death a year ago had been almost too much to bear.

Still Leith said nothing. His silence was beginning to irk her. She was qualified for the job—more than qualified—so what more did he need to know? Was the thought of working with her so distasteful to him? She rose to her feet. 'I'm sorry. Maybe this job isn't right for me after all. I suspect you are looking for someone with more general practice experience. Thank you for your time.'

'Please, sit down, Dr Ross,' Leith drawled,

sounding almost bored. 'In a practice such as this it is important that we are all clear where individual skills lie. Your references are all first class. And I remember your work on board the Mercy Ship. It couldn't be faulted.'

Cassie took a breath and sat back down. Perhaps she was being overly sensitive? Seeing Leith again had been a bigger shock than she'd expected.

'I see your last posting was in Afghanistan,' Rose said. 'Could you tell us a little about that?'

Cassie's heart thumped sickeningly.

'I went out there on my second secondment with the UN. My job was to treat the children of the civilian population as part of the initiative to win hearts and minds. Medical services for the civilian population are suffering badly and it is the children who suffer most.'

Both Rose and Leith were listening attentively.

'I was there for nine months,' she said, choosing her words carefully. This part was easy. She forced herself to look at Leith. 'In many ways it wasn't very different to working on the Mercy Ship—or in Sudan. We held clinics where we could and even went into the hospitals to see patients if we were asked.' She didn't mention that each visit had required the presence of soldiers in order to protect her and the other members of the medical team.

'If we found a child who required surgery beyond what we could offer locally—as you can imagine, equipment was pretty basic if it existed at all—we sent the children to the UK or the US for treatment. Sadly there is often a far greater demand than can be provided.'

Rose turned to Leith. 'There must be something we could do to help.' Rose must have noticed Cassie's confusion as she smiled. 'We all feel incredibly fortunate to lead the lives we do so it's the ethos of our practice that we all do voluntary work for two to three weeks every year—either locally or abroad. And it's possible we could find surgeons here in Britain who would be prepared to help the children you talk about.' She smiled. 'My husband has many contacts and he's not beyond twisting an arm if he needs to.'

Cassie smiled back. She liked Rose already. 'That would be fantastic.'

'I must tell you that our doctors are required

to travel occasionally. Will that be a problem?' Rose continued.

'Not at all,' Cassie replied. 'I don't have ties to keep me in London.' She was acutely aware of Leith's silence.

Rose beamed at her, looking relieved. 'That is good news. We all try to do our fair share of the trips abroad but as some of us have children...' she glanced at Leith before sending Cassie another smile '...we prefer to stay at home if we can.'

So it seemed Leith had managed to gain access to his child. She wasn't surprised.

'I don't care what I do or where I go as long as I'm working.' When Rose and Leith exchanged another glance she rushed on. 'I like to work.'

'And what do you do in your spare time?' Rose asked. Leith leaned forward, staring at her intently. She shifted under his gaze.

'I run. I...' She hesitated, lifting the hair from the back of her neck. 'I like the theatre, going out to dinner, that sort of thing.' It wasn't altogether a lie. That *was* what she used to like to do.

'The practice is expanding almost faster than we can cope with,' Rose said. 'When I first came here there was only my husband and a couple of nurses. But in the last two years we have taken over the building next door and installed a minor surgery unit as well as full X-ray facilities. We have grown from a single-handed practice to three doctors and are continuing to expand. With Fabio planning to take time off, we badly need another doctor to see the children. By most standards we're a small practice but we're a happy one and we want to keep it that way. Everyone has to get on. And if our questions seem a little—er—searching that's because it's important that we all get along.' She smiled again.

'The other reason our questions might seem intrusive is because of the patients we deal with. They can be anyone from royalty to politicians, people in the media and sports stars. All of them rely on our absolute discretion. So our checks have to be thorough. I'm sure you understand.'

Cassie let her breath out slowly. Until now she hadn't been aware of how tense she'd been. Tiredness was making her defensive. Of course they were only doing what anyone would do when they were looking to take on new staff.

They weren't to know how much she hated answering personal questions. And she did need this job. Even if the thought of working alongside Leith, who appeared to have turned into Dr See-Right-Through-You-and-Not-Sure-I-Approve, worried her.

'Dr Ballantyne and the other doctors also spend some time at the local hospital,' Rose said. 'You would have access to the facilities there if needed.'

'Sounds perfect,' Cassie replied. At least, the job *would* be perfect if it weren't for the fact that she'd be working with Leith.

This time it was Rose who stood and held out her hand. 'We have a couple of other applicants to consider and naturally any decisions we make will be made after discussions with the rest of the team.'

'When will you let me know?' Cassie was relieved to find her voice was steady, betraying none of the anxiety she felt at being turned down. She simply could not spend any more time not working. She would truly go mad.

'By tomorrow evening at the latest,' Rose promised.

* * *

'So, what do you think?' Rose asked when Cassie had left the room. Leith wasn't sure how to answer. Cassie was a top-class doctor. Almost too qualified for the job on offer. And what had really made her apply for this post? He didn't find her explanations totally convincing.

Seeing Cassie again had been like a punch in his solar plexus. So much for thinking he was completely over her.

Yet she'd changed. She was still beautiful, perhaps even more than he'd remembered, but distant—as if she wasn't really connecting. Her hair was longer, at times hiding her face, and she was thin, almost to the point of gauntness. And it wasn't just her physical appearance that had altered. Somewhere along the way she'd lost the fire in her eyes and she seemed almost…lost. At least, that's what he would have said if it didn't seem fanciful.

What had changed her? The death of someone close to her would account for some of the sadness but this seemed deeper than normal grief. Had something happened while she'd been working in Afghanistan? Had she seen things that had eaten away at her? Or was he reading too much into her manner towards him? Perhaps she was simply uncomfortable coming face to face with him? She needn't worry. He had no intention of resurrecting a past affair. An affair that had clearly meant little to her.

But hell. Despite everything, she still made him want to hold her. He couldn't stop himself from thinking of her naked body moving beneath his; the way she'd cried out when they'd made love; the way she'd felt in his arms. And not just that. He wanted to banish the aching sadness from her eyes—see her face light up with a smile and hear her laugh again.

Was he nuts? Completely out of his mind? He'd been mistaken about her before and his life was too complicated now to want her back in it again.

He became aware that Rose was looking at him, expecting an answer.

'I wonder about her commitment. This job doesn't seem to fit with what I know of her. Not that I knew her that well,' he added quickly. Hadn't known her at all, if the truth be told. He'd never thought she'd leave the way she had, with a casualness that had stunned him and making it abundantly clear she'd had no desire to pursue their relationship. But he'd been so focussed on getting his son that he hadn't thought about her—at least, not that much.

'Well, I liked her,' Rose said. 'I think she's perfect for the job.'

Could he work with Cassie again? They were both adults and, as he kept telling himself, whatever had been between them was in the past. So why was he hesitating? Cassie *was* well qualified, far more than any of the other applicants they had interviewed, and if Rose had taken a shine to her, he trusted her judgement completely.

'If you like her, I'm sure Jonathan will,' Leith replied. 'And we do need someone to take over the paediatric side for a bit. But let's wait until we hear what the others have to say. And we also have the other applicants to consider.'

'Yes, but neither of us were really taken with them, were we?' Rose chewed on her lower lip. 'I think we should offer her the job. I've a good feeling about her.'

Leith shrugged. 'Fine by me, as long as Jonathan agrees.'

Rose slid him a mischievous look. 'You know Jonathan trusts my judgement completely. And you're happy with her medical qualifications. Surely that counts more than anything?'

If Rose knew the true extent of his relationship with Cassie perhaps she'd understand his reluctance. However, that had nothing to do with whether she was qualified for this position. This was, he reminded himself, a purely professional decision. 'Okay, you win,' he said with as much nonchalance as he could muster. 'Dr Ross it is.'

'I've just had the most perfect idea,' Rose said as she gathered up her papers. 'Why don't I invite Cassie to our gathering at Cavendish Hall at the weekend? It will be so much more relaxing for her to meet everyone when they're off duty and we can all get a chance to know her. What do think, Leith?'

Seeing Rose's delighted face, Leith didn't have the heart to tell her that he very much doubted that Cassie would find being sized up over a weekend at Cavendish Hall relaxing. It was a sensible plan, though. 'I think it's a great idea, although you should ring her as soon as possible to give her some warning.'

So it seemed that, whether he liked it or not, Cassie was back in his life.

CHAPTER FOUR

CASSIE WOKE HERSELF up with her cries. Praying that the sound hadn't carried through the walls of her flat and disturbed her neighbours, she waited in the darkness until her heart rate slowed and she was able to breathe normally.

It was the same nightmare she had every night. She'd be walking along when suddenly a fireball would come from nowhere. She would fall to the ground and listen to the calls for help. But when she tried to move she couldn't. Then she'd look down and notice that her right side was on fire. It was horrible. Even worse in some respects than the reality.

Although it was only just after six a.m., it was already light outside. Slipping on her sweats and a T-shirt, she let herself out of her flat and started running in the direction of Hyde Park.

Would the practice phone today and offer her the job? And if they did, was she seriously going to say yes? She'd been dismayed—more than dismayed, horrified—at the way her heart had thumped when she'd seen Leith again. Maybe working with him wasn't such a good idea. On the other hand, perhaps she should think of her reaction to him as a good sign. It meant she wasn't totally dead inside.

He, to her chagrin, hadn't looked fazed in the slightest. Had he met someone else? He hadn't been wearing a ring, but many men didn't. The thought of him being married made her insides churn and she picked up speed, pushing herself to go faster—almost as if she could outrun her thoughts. And what about his son? Was he living with Leith? She shook her head. Leith and his child were none of her business. It was as much as she could manage to get herself through each day.

The unaccustomed exertion was making her chest ache. Once she could have done twice this distance without any difficulty but weeks of inactivity following her hospital stay had made her muscles lazy and her lungs underperform.

She was gasping for breath by the time she returned to her flat. She pulled the T-shirt over her head and stepped out of her jogging pants before throwing them in the laundry bin. She looked around the flat. Everything was in its place—just the way she liked it. She ignored the niggling unease in the back of her mind that her preferred level of tidiness was not normal. But, she told herself, it wasn't doing any harm and it made her feel in control.

On her way to the bathroom she noticed the red light of her answering-machine flashing. She hadn't checked for messages before going to bed last night. She picked up the phone and pressed the 'retrieve messages' symbol. She recognised the voice straight away. It was Rose Cavendish, asking her if she could ring her back as soon as she got a chance.

Cavendish Hall was a ninety-minute drive from London and Cassie left her arrival as late as she dared. She really didn't know how she was going to manage to get through the next twenty-four hours. Rose had been vague about what she should bring—some stout boots and a waterproof, otherwise just the usual.

From the rare times her adoptive parents had

taken her with them when they'd gone to stay with their friends, Cassie knew that guests at house parties in grand houses normally dressed for dinner, so she had packed the one evening dress she had with long enough sleeves to cover the scars on her arms. If it wasn't fancy enough for dinner, that was too bad. There was no time to go shopping for another one. Once upon a time she had enjoyed scouring the shops for the latest fashions but these days she had little energy or interest for it.

The same could be said for a lot of things she'd once enjoyed. She gave herself a mental shake. Hadn't she promised herself that, instead of letting what had happened to her ruin her life, she was going to make the most of this second chance she'd been given? She had made a start by applying for this job. And if her head couldn't quite shake off the past, she would simply have to try harder.

As she turned into the long, sweeping drive, passing a gatehouse on her right, Cavendish Hall appeared before her. The double-storey, honey-coloured sandstone building was much larger than Cassie had expected, with what had to be at least a dozen Georgian windows facing out over a sizeable manicured lawn.

Rose was waiting at the bottom of steps, watching a little girl dousing some flowers with a watering-can almost as large as herself, with the affection that only a mother could have. Some things would never change, Cassie thought ruefully, though she still couldn't see herself with children.

Rose's face broke into a wide smile when Cassie brought her rental car to a halt. She'd hardly had a chance to take her overnight case from the boot when Rose hurried towards her with her arms held wide, enveloped her in a hug and kissed her warmly on the cheeks. The little girl came to stand next to her mother, studying Cassie with wide eyes.

'Welcome to Cavendish Hall,' Rose said. 'I'm so glad you could make it on such short notice. The others have all arrived and are looking forward to meeting you. I hope you don't mind being dragged out here to meet everyone.'

Cassie's head was beginning to ache. 'No, of course not.'

'Now, we're quite informal here. Not like in

Jonathan's father's day. Poor man passed away two years ago—he was a darling when you got to know him, although he was a bit fierce to me at first. Once Daisy came along, he melted like a marshmallow. Oh, forgive me—I always talk too much.' She bent her head to whisper in Cassie's ear, 'I still get nervous when I have to be hostess.'

For the first time in as long as she could remember, Cassie laughed. There was something so straightforward and down to earth about Rose Cavendish that Cassie couldn't help but warm to her.

'Katie, the practice physio, is inside and dying to meet you. Poor thing is huge and feels the heat. She's thirty-six weeks pregnant with her first child, you know. Oh, of course you don't. Well, she is.' As Rose had been talking she'd taken Cassie by the arm and was leading her up the stone steps.

'Jonathan and Fabio—that's the doctor you'll be covering for and Katie's husband—and Leith are out in the grounds somewhere, looking at fences or whatever it is that men do. They'll be back shortly, no doubt, in search of tea and some of Mary's home baking.' She looked down at her child, who was tugging at her dress.

'This little scamp is Daisy.'

Daisy held out a small, plump hand and Cassie shook it solemnly.

'And this is Benton—without whom Cavendish Hall would likely fall to the ground.'

Benton, clearly well past the first bloom of youth, harrumphed dismissively but the look he gave Rose was one of pure adoration.

'Actually, Benton, could you go and find Jonathan and let him know Dr Ross has arrived?' Rose asked.

Cassie looked around for her bag but Benton had already picked it up and was following them up the steps. He stooped to pick up the little girl and with the ease of a man half his age swung her onto his shoulders. Then, before Cassie could wonder if she'd stepped into a children's story book, she was in the drawing room and being introduced to Katie—a striking woman with thick blonde hair and large grey eyes.

'Please don't get up,' Cassie said hastily, as Katie struggled to ease her bulk from the deep, overstuffed arm chair.

'Thanks. I won't then. Particularly as it takes me about ten minutes to get on my feet. Rose, couldn't you find one chair that doesn't feel as if it is swallowing me whole?' The last was said with an affectionate grin at their hostess and Cassie relaxed a little more.

'Rose tells me you're around thirty-six weeks,' Cassie said. 'You must be excited.'

'Excited?' Katie widened her eyes and gave Cassie a mischievous grin. 'More like bored, fed up, huge, terrified, I'm afraid. Nobody warned me I'd feel like a beached whale at this point.' Katie cradled her stomach with her hands. 'And look like one too.'

'But, my darling, you look as beautiful as ever. Even more beautiful if that's possible.' A good-looking man with an olive complexion strode into the room and dropped a kiss on Katie's cheek.

The gesture was so full of love and affection that Cassie felt her throat tighten. What would it be like to be loved like that? She glanced over to the door and her heart banged painfully. Leith was leaning against the doorjamb, watching her, sexy as hell in dark jeans and a muscle-defining sage-green T-shirt. Damn. Whatever she told herself, she was still in lust. Quickly she composed her features and looked away. She didn't want him to see her reaction.

Katie swatted her husband playfully. 'Cassie, this is my husband, Fabio.'

Next to Fabio was another dark-haired man who, judging by his resemblance to Daisy, had to be Jonathan.

Was Leith on his own? No girlfriend? And where was his little boy? Hadn't he managed to get access after all—or had he just given up?

'Welcome to Cavendish Hall,' Jonathan echoed his wife's greeting, although his voice was much more public school than Rose's. 'I hope you have everything you need.'

'I haven't had the chance to show her to her room, darling. I'll do that after we've had some tea. I've put you in the west wing next to Leith. I thought you might like to be out of hearing of Daisy, who can make quite a racket when she's excited, I'm afraid. I hope that's okay?'

Despite her promise to herself not to, Cassie couldn't help glancing at Leith. For a moment their eyes locked. When he grinned, her stomach lurched. Curse her libido to have chosen this time to resurface.

'Anywhere is fine. And I'm happy to wait until later to unpack—although I wouldn't mind a chance to freshen up.' The truth was she wanted a few minutes away from Leith to collect herself.

When Rose showed her to the downstairs bathroom, Cassie leaned against the door and took deep breaths before crossing over to the sink and splashing cool water on her neck. For heaven's sake, she chided herself, get a grip.

By the time she returned to the drawing room, tea was being poured and the room was filled with the sound of lively chatter. She paused just inside the doorway, feeling isolated. How would it be to feel a sense of belonging instead of always feeling like an outsider? To laugh and chat as if nothing else mattered but being in the moment—at ease with people who accepted you for who you were, and without judgement.

'Are you all right?'

She jumped. She hadn't been aware of Leith coming to stand next to her.

'Of course,' she replied. 'Why shouldn't I be?'

He looked down at her, his dark green eyes

puzzled. 'I don't know. But something tells me you're not comfortable. I imagine as a group we can be a little overwhelming at first.'

'I'm not very good with large numbers of people if you remember,' she said at last.

A strange look crossed his face. 'I remember everything, Cassie. Trust me, there was nothing forgettable about you.' Her nerve endings thrummed like a still-vibrating guitar string.

'Why don't we get out of here for a bit? 'He nodded towards the group of her soon-to-be colleagues. Rose and Jonathan were reading to Daisy, and Katie and Fabio had their heads close together as they shared a joke 'They won't mind.' There was a faint glimmer of a smile in his eyes. 'I doubt they'll even notice. Besides…' he lowered his voice '…we should talk.'

'I don't think there's anything to talk about,' Cassie whispered back. Thankfully, the others didn't appear to be paying them any attention. 'We worked together some months ago. Had a short shipboard romance. Isn't that all there is to say on the matter?' She shrugged, hoping she looked and sounded way more blasé than she was feeling.

He studied her through narrowed eyes. Then he took her by the elbow and steered her though the open French windows and out to the patio. There was little she could do about it without drawing the attention of everyone in the room. Besides, sooner or later they would have to talk so she might as well get it over with. And she was curious to know about his son.

As soon as they were outside she shook his arm from her elbow. They walked in silence for a while, following a path that led towards a small copse on the edge of the estate. The air between them shivered with tension.

'Why did you come back to London?' Leith asked abruptly. 'It must have been a blow to give up your position with the United Nations. If I remember correctly, you were determined to stay with them for the foreseeable future. So determined you didn't even leave me your contact number. Only a note. And a brief one at that.'

'I'm sorry. I thought it was better that way.'

'Hell, Cassie, I thought we meant more to each other than that. I couldn't believe you left without coming to find me.'

'And as I said in my letter, I hate goodbyes. We

both knew there wasn't a future in it. You had your son and I...well, I had my job with the UN.'

'The job you've now given up. And, if I remember correctly, we agreed to keep in touch. What changed?' His voice was ominously quiet.

She pretended to misunderstand him. 'As I mentioned at the interview, someone close to me died and left me her flat. I needed to sort it before I put it on the market.'

'You haven't answered my question, Cassie.'

'It was pointless to keep in touch. Surely you could see that? We were only together for a short while, Leith. You had your life and I had mine.' She dragged in a breath. 'I didn't want to be held to vague promises that we both knew would be difficult to keep.' She forced lightness into her voice she was far from feeling. 'I wanted to go to Sudan as a free agent. Months apart was never going to work—for either of us.'

'You never gave it a try, Cassie.' He shook his head. 'Of course, now I can see you were right. What we had was...good, but it seems neither of us was the person the other one thought we were. As you say, what happened back in Africa is in the past.' His eyes were guarded.

'But to give up your career with the United Nations? Surely you could have sorted the flat during your leave? Or handed it to someone else to do? Or was there another reason you left?' He looked her in the eyes. 'Or someone else?'

Her heart was beating so fast she felt nauseous. 'No, there's been no one...' She swallowed. 'It was just time for me to move on. As far as leaving Martha's flat for someone else to sort out...' When her voice hitched, she took a deep breath. 'She was someone I cared deeply about. I owed it to her to do this one last thing for her.'

'I'm sorry. I didn't realise...Was she a good friend?' The sympathy in his voice made her throat tighten.

'You could say that. But she was getting on in years and in the end, although her death was sudden, at least she didn't suffer. She would have hated to have become dependent on anyone.' She needed to change the subject. Martha was part of the life she didn't want Leith to know about. She took a breath to steady her voice. 'But what about you? Are you with someone? Married? And what happened with Peter?'

Her chest tightened as Leith continued to study

her for a long moment. He shook his head. 'No, I'm not married.'

A wave of relief washed over her. Even if they couldn't be together, she hated the thought of him being with anyone else.

'As for gaining access to Peter,' he continued, 'that hasn't gone quite as smoothly as I thought. First I had to prove I was his biological father. Then I had to get Social Services involved.' His expression darkened. 'To be honest, it's been a mess. I've met him once or twice at his grandmother's house. I can't say it was a huge success. My son seems to hate me.'

Cassie was appalled. The very thing she had warned Leith about had happened. Poor mite. However bad his mother, it would have been a wrench to be taken from her.

And as for Leith, his son's rejection must have been a blow.

She touched his arm. 'I'm sure he just needs time to get to know you.'

'Jude's mother and sister keep in touch with me and are the only way I know what's happening with him. Not having him with me, I can't help worrying whether he's okay. They say Jude's behaviour is getting more erratic. Her mother has him living with her now, with Jude having supervised access. At least until custody's decided.' Leith's eyes were bleak. 'Damn a system that takes so long to decide a child's future.'

The system hadn't worked for her either. The poor little boy. He'd never know how his mother would behave from one day to the next. Cassie's heart ached for him—and Leith. 'It's good that Peter has people who love him and are watching out for him. Perhaps Jude could be persuaded to go to rehab? Wouldn't that be best for everyone?'

'Jude has been to rehab before—without success. I have just about persuaded her mother and sister to go to court and admit that Jude has a drug problem,' Leith said tightly. 'Understandably they are worried that if they do, Jude will lose access to Peter altogether and they'll lose touch with her. Personally I don't care. I just want my son here with me, where he'll be safe.'

Unfortunately, there was more to it than that. Cassie often wondered what would have happened if her mother hadn't died and she hadn't been taken into foster-care. Perhaps her mother would have found some way of getting back control of her life and with it her daughter. At least, for all her mother's faults she had loved her. It had been an erratic, careless love, but at the end of the day it had been more than her adoptive mother had been able to give.

'Isn't it better that he maintains some contact with his mother?' she ventured tentatively. 'With the grandmother and sister keeping an eye on things?'

Leith looked incredulous. 'You can't mean that!'

'It can't be doing your son any good to be fought over.'

'I want sole custody. I won't stop him from seeing his mother, I just want to make sure that my son is safe and that whenever he's with his mother it's under supervision. By her actions, Jude has given up the right to care for Peter. Surely, as a paediatrician, you must agree that being with me would be best for him?'

It might have been her professional opinion, but it would never be her personal one. Her head was beginning to ache again. Wasn't this one of the reasons she'd decided she and Leith could never be together? She'd spent too much time getting herself together to risk becoming involved in someone else's life—particularly his.

'If you don't mind,' she said, 'I think I'll go back to the house and unpack.'

As she turned, he gripped her by the arm. 'Why *did* you apply for the job, Cassie? With your track record you could have taken a job anywhere.'

She looked at him steadily. 'It wasn't anything to do with you, in case you're wondering. As I said before, this job suits me. I'm a good doctor, Leith. Patients like me. I'll do anything and go anywhere. As far as I'm concerned, that's all that matters.' She raised an eyebrow and smiled again. 'I promise I won't let you down. At least—' she dropped her voice '—I'll do my damnedest not to.'

Cassie was grateful to reach the privacy of her room without encountering the others. Leith was far too perceptive for her liking. He'd guessed she'd hadn't been telling the whole truth about why she'd left the United Nations but, thank God, she'd managed to divert him. However, she suspected that one way or another he wouldn't be satisfied until he knew everything. Damn. He had no right to probe into her life. Whatever there had been between them was over.

At least they had talked. Even if it had been like two casual acquaintances. That was good. It kept everything on a professional footing and would make working together easier.

She unpacked the few items she'd brought with her and hung her clothes in the ornate mahogany wardrobe. She had to admit she loved the room she'd been given. It was distinctly old-fashioned but she liked the high double bed and slightly worn carpet. This house had history and she could almost sense the presence of generations who had lived here. What would it be like to know who your family was, going back through time?

Slipping out of her dress and into her dressing gown, she went in search of the bathroom. Rose had apologised when she'd pointed it out at the end of the corridor. They had, she'd said, hoped to upgrade Cavendish Hall, but were tackling major jobs—like a new roof for one of the wings first. And with a smile she'd added that with a small, lively child and a job, it wasn't high on her list of priorities.

Cassie liked Rose and Jonathan Cavendish as well as what she'd seen of the Linehams. If things had been different, perhaps she could even have been friends with Rose and Katie. But she didn't do friends.

She immersed herself in the enormous claw-foot bath and closed her eyes. It all felt like such an effort. It was as if lately she'd had a shell around her that muffled everything. She suspected she was probably suffering from a mild form of post-traumatic stress disorder, but that didn't make any of it easier to bear.

She'd considered going to a psychologist but the thought of having to talk to someone about what had happened—about her life—made her feel nauseous. No, she would get through this by herself. One day at a time. Keep busy. And work—caring for others—and not having time to think about her past was the best remedy.

She eased herself out of the bath and once she was dry she wrapped herself in her dressing gown.

Halfway down the corridor she was alarmed

to see Leith walking towards her. He was naked, apart from a towel knotted loosely around his hips. Immediately the memory of his naked chest under her fingertips flooded back and the nerve endings on her skin tingled. She averted her gaze, but not before she'd seen the gleam of amusement in his eyes.

'The bathroom is that way,' she said, pointing behind her.

'Thank you. I have been here before.'

As the corridor was narrow she had to slide past him. She pressed herself so hard against the wall she could have made a dent. She raised her hand, almost as if she would push him away, but as she did so the sleeve of her dressing gown rode up.

'What the hell...?' Leith took her arm and turned it to catch the light.

'It's nothing...an accident.' When she tried to pull away he tightened his grip.

'It must have been some accident!' He ran the pad of his thumb over the scars. 'This would have taken months to heal.'

She wrenched her arm away. 'Please, Leith, it's not something I want to talk about. Let me past.'

'Damn it, Cassie, what is it you're not telling me?' he growled. When she shook her head he lowered his voice. 'You know you can trust me. I'm still your friend.'

'Really, there's nothing I need—or want—to talk about.'

He hesitated, before reaching up to push a lock of wet hair from her eyes. 'You know where to find me when you're ready,' he said softly, before stepping aside to let her pass.

As she fumbled with the handle of the door to her room Cassie was uncomfortably aware that his puzzled gaze had followed her down the corridor.

By the time she had dressed and come downstairs, everyone had assembled in the drawing room. To her mortification she was overdressed in her floor-length, long-sleeved blue gown. The heat rose in her cheeks as everyone turned to look at her.

'Cassie, how lovely you look,' said Rose, hurrying forward and taking her by the hands. 'My goodness, you're freezing and we haven't lit a fire.'

'It *is* the middle of summer,' Cassie responded lightly. Indeed, the late evening sunshine was flooding the room, making the dust motes dance. Leith was standing on the other side of the room, his hands wrapped around his drink. For a second their gazes locked and once again she had the sensation of the ground shifting beneath her. Quickly she glanced away, focussing her attention instead on the glass of champagne Jonathan pressed into her hands.

Katie was ensconced in an armchair, with Fabio sitting on the arm next to her. Daisy was nowhere to be seen. She would, no doubt, be tucked up in bed for the night.

'What shall we do tomorrow, darling?' Jonathan asked his wife. 'I thought I might take Leith and Fabio out on the estate and do some clay-pigeon shooting.' He looked at Cassie. 'Would you like to join us, Cassie? Katie doesn't care to be on her feet, and Rose will want to be with Daisy, but you might like to come along.'

'I was intending to come, too,' Rose protested. 'Vicki and Julie—our nurses—will be joining us, and Jenny, our receptionist, too. Unfortunately, none of them could manage tonight. I thought we could all picnic down by the lake.'

'That's settled, then,' Jonathan said.

'I'm sorry,' Cassie said. 'I meant to let you know sooner but I have to leave early tomorrow. A previous arrangement in London I forgot to mention.' She simply could not go through a whole day in Leith's company. Working with him would be bad enough.

'That's too bad,' Rose said. 'But we're all so glad you managed to come for the night. Particularly on such short notice.'

From somewhere deep in the house a gong rang. 'That's Mrs Hammond, our housekeeper, letting us know dinner is ready. Shall we go through? Leith, perhaps you'll escort Cassie?'

Her heart rate upped another notch when Leith took her arm. It was as if she'd been catapulted into another time, Cassie thought distractedly as Jonathan led the way into an enormous dining room. The table, lit by several candles, was laid with sparkling crystal and fine china.

Rose, noting her look, smiled wryly. 'Jonathan's father liked to keep dinner the way it always was in his time. Since his death, we've kept up the practice.'

'I've never socialised with a lord and lady before,' Cassie replied, completely unable to think of anything else to say. She could still feel the warmth of Leith's fingertips through the sleeve of her dress and it had taken all her self-control not to yank it from his grip. But when he relinquished her arm to pull out a chair for her, she felt almost bereft.

Everyone laughed. 'You'll find that Rose and Jonathan don't care for their titles,' Katie said. 'I've never met anyone less like the lady of the manor than Rose!'

'Katie!' Rose responded. 'You've hurt me to the quick.' But her eyes were dancing. She turned to Cassie, who had been seated, to her consternation, directly opposite Leith. Now there would be no escape from his piercing gaze. 'I was born to loving but very ordinary parents. I grew up on a council estate outside London. I can't quite believe that I am Lady Cavendish. What about you, Cassie? Where do you come from?'

Cassie almost groaned. She should have refused the invitation to the weekend. She was certain to have found another job somewhere else. But she was here now and Rose was only being polite after all. Nevertheless, she had to force herself not to look at Leith.

'My father works for a bank and my mother—she's in the media.'

'A journalist?' Fabio asked.

'Not exactly,' Cassie admitted. 'She is—was—a war correspondent.'

'Good grief,' Jonathan said. 'What's her name?'

'Lily,' Cassie admitted. 'She uses her maiden name—Savage.' Savage by name. Savage by nature.

'You're Lily Savage's daughter?' Rose said, her eyes wide. 'I had no idea she even had children.'

That was hardly surprising.

'She doesn't cover war zones any more,' Cassie said. 'She mainly does documentaries.'

'Oh, what a coincidence,' Katie said. 'Fabio's mother is also in the media. He knows all about being the child of famous parents—don't you, darling?'

Fabio glanced at Cassie and smiled wryly. 'I know it's not always easy.'

The sympathy in his eyes made her throat

tighten. She'd only been around these people for a few hours and already they were treating her as if she was someone they cared about. The thought panicked her. She took a deep breath.

'No, it's not always easy.' She lifted her eyes to Leith, unsurprised to find his gaze on her. She couldn't read the expression in his eyes. 'How are your parents, Leith?'

'The same as always. And I'm glad that no one can say that my upbringing was anything but ordinary. I was brought up on a small croft on Skye by two loving but relatively skint parents.'

'Didn't hold you back, did it?' Katie said with a smile.

'Quite the opposite,' Leith said. 'They taught me to believe that a person can be whatever he or she wants to be—as long as they have self-belief.'

Rose raised her glass. 'I'll drink to that. I also have a great deal to thank my parents for.'

Cassie's heart squeezed. At that moment she envied Rose—and Leith—with all her being.

'What about you, Katie?'

'Nope. No famous parents either. Fabio has it all on his side.' She closed her eyes for a moment and Cassie saw pain wash across her face. 'I did have a brother. He was a doctor in the army. He was killed in Iraq just over a year ago.'

Nausea swelled in Cassie's abdomen. In her head she heard explosions—saw flying dirt—and then that eerie silence that was almost worse than anything that had gone before.

'Are you okay, Cassie?' She was aware of Leith's voice coming as if from a distance. She gave herself a mental shake. She simply couldn't lose it! Not here. She looked at Katie, noticing that Fabio had reached over to take his wife's hand. 'I'm so sorry, Katie,' Cassie said. She forced herself to take a mouthful of whatever was on her plate. What was it anyway? She couldn't tell. Her mouth was so dry she doubted she'd manage to swallow.

'Perhaps we should talk about something else,' Leith said quickly, and to her relief they moved on to discussing patients. Cassie concentrated on trying to get her heart rate down, nodding and smiling in what she hoped were the right places.

Eventually dinner came to an end and they rose from the table.

'Would you think me very rude if I went to bed?' Cassie asked. 'I'm afraid I have a bit of a headache.'

Five pairs of concerned eyes turned her way, but before they could say anything, Cassie smiled vaguely at no one in particular and fled.

Safely back in her room, Cassie paced the floor. Of all the people she could have chosen to look for a job alongside, it had to be this lot. It wasn't that they were unkind—quite the opposite. Their friendliness was genuine and that was the problem.

Cassie didn't want to form attachments. She remembered leaving the Mercy Ship. It hadn't been just leaving without saying goodbye to Leith that had been a wrench. She had tried to slip away but some of the nurses had got up early so that they could see her off and their hugs and entreaties to stay in touch had moved her. She'd only been there for two short weeks yet they'd made it clear that they saw her as part of their 'family'.

And then there were the staff she'd worked with in Afghanistan. She'd allowed herself to get close to them too—and that had brought her nothing but agony. No. It was far better not to get involved. That way no one got hurt—at least, not emotionally.

As for Leith, almost eighteen months had passed and he still made her heart pound. Now he looked at her as if he had never made love to her with an intensity that had taken both their breaths away.

But if she wouldn't let him love her back then she was even less likely to let him love her now. The woman he'd thought he'd cared for no longer existed—if she ever did—and he would find that out soon enough. She rubbed her aching temples. The headache hadn't been a lie.

No doubt the team would be thinking she had a screw loose and perhaps they were right. Perhaps they were even having second thoughts about hiring her. She could still turn the position down and sign up with a locum agency instead. Almost as soon as the thought came into her head, she dismissed it. Hadn't she promised herself she'd get on with her life? If the practice was happy to have her, she would make sure they never regretted it.

* * *

'So what do we think?' Rose said. 'Have we done the right thing in offering Cassie the job? Oh, do stop pacing, Leith, and come and sit down.'

Leith did as she asked. Cassie was behaving oddly, there was no doubt. He'd noticed her reaction when Katie had talked about her brother's death. Then there were those scars on the inside of her arm. Those were the result of a serious accident. Exactly what secrets did Cassie have? What was she not telling him? And, more importantly, why?

'I think we have,' Jonathan said, looking puzzled. 'We need another doctor and she's more than qualified.'

'I'm happy,' Fabio said. 'I'll be taking paternity leave in a week or two and we'll be short-staffed. We need someone with her skills and experience to take on the paediatric side.'

'No second thoughts, Leith?' Rose looked at him and raised an eyebrow. 'You know her best.'

'As I've said, she was a fine doctor when I knew her on the Mercy Ship,' he said honestly. 'One of the best. No one had anything but praise for her.' He pushed his doubts aside. Whatever alarm bells were going off in his head about Cassie had nothing to do with her medical ability and he shouldn't let his personal feelings cloud his judgement. They did need someone to take over from Fabio and it would only be for a few weeks. 'I voted yes and I'm sticking to it.'

Jonathan got to his feet. 'In that case, we're agreed. Ask her to start on Monday. That way she can get to know some of my patients before I have to hand over their care.'

As everyone trooped out of the room on their way to bed, Leith remained standing by the window. Cassie was back in his life and he wasn't at all sure that was a good thing.

Cassie was dreaming again. This time she was standing in a field. At first she thought she was all alone. She knew there were bombs and that she couldn't move right or left. She would have to stay exactly where she was until someone rescued her.

Then she heard it. The sound of someone sobbing. It was coming from her left. It looked like a pile of rags but she knew it wasn't. It was Linda.

She was hurt and Cassie had to get to her. But her legs wouldn't obey her.

Linda got to her feet and staggered. Cassie tried to call out to her—to tell her to stay where she was, that help was on the way—but the words wouldn't come. Almost in slow motion Cassie saw Linda turn. A smile of relief crossed her face and she lifted her foot and started to walk towards Cassie.

Cassie found her voice. 'No!' she screamed.

Leith jumped out of bed, unsure of what he'd heard. Had it been the cry of a fox or an owl? He wandered over to the window and looked out, his ears straining for the sound.

The large gardens of Cavendish Hall were in semi-darkness. At this time of year it didn't get truly dark until much later and then only for a brief time.

He thought of the evening that had passed. It had been strange spending time in Cassie's company after all these months. Strange—and unsettling.

It wasn't as if he hadn't thought of her since they'd parted. He had, and too often for his peace of mind. He'd thought of trying to track her down several times, but at the last minute he'd always changed his mind. Between the court case and work there had been little time for anything else—even if Cassie hadn't made it clear that whatever had happened between them on the Mercy Ship had just been a way of passing time.

And—speak of the devil—there she was. At first she'd been just a shape in the moonlit night until his eyes had adjusted to the darkness and she'd moved.

What was she doing outside and at this time of night?

Despite the way she seemed to have changed, she still had the same effect on him. His senses still came alert whenever she was near. His stomach clenched as images of her in his arms forced their way into his head.

Back on the Mercy Ship he'd started to believe he'd found the only woman he could even imagine having a future with and then…well, if she hadn't made it clear she didn't feel the same, there was Peter. But now she was back in his life and although he wasn't at all sure that that was a good thing, he had to deal with it.

He narrowed his eyes to see better. She was leaning against a tree, the back of her head pressed against the trunk. There was something in the slump of her shoulders, the despair in the tilt of her neck that sent a flicker of alarm up his spine.

Quickly he stepped into his jeans and pulled a thin sweater over his head. Not bothering with shoes, he ran quietly down the stairs, took a torch from the table in the hall and let himself out of the heavy front door.

His bare feet made no sound on the grass and he was almost upon her when she looked up. Her eyes widened for a moment and even in the dim light he thought he saw relief and something else he couldn't name in her expression, but then she straightened and blinked and he knew he must have been mistaken.

'Oh, it's you,' she said flatly. 'What are you doing out at this time?'

'I could ask the same of you,' he murmured.

'I couldn't sleep,' she said. 'I thought a walk might help.'

He showed her the torch. 'A walk sounds good. There's a path that leads around to the summer pavilion. Unless you knew it was there, you'd never suspect there was one.'

She hesitated and looked towards the house as if about to refuse, but then she smiled faintly. 'We always did seem to meet more often in the dark,' she said finally. Then her smile grew broader and he caught a glimpse of the Cassie he'd once known—or thought he'd known. 'Been attacked by any more giant spiders recently?' she teased.

He grinned back. 'No, but I'd be grateful if you didn't let the rest know about my failing.'

'My lips are sealed,' she replied, falling into step beside him.

'I hope this evening wasn't too nerve-racking,' he said. Although the Cassie he'd known wouldn't have let meeting a few strangers affect her, she'd always seemed to prefer her own company or— on the Mercy Ship—his.

'Everyone was lovely,' Cassie replied. 'I don't imagine anyone would mind working with them.'

Then what? Leith wondered. Something had upset her at dinner. He would have bet his life on it. She had been like a cat on a hot tin roof all evening—oh, she'd disguised it well but he had sensed her unease and then, when Katie had spoken about her brother, Cassie had paled. And there were the scars. Something had happened in Afghanistan. Something bad. His stomach clenched. He bit back the temptation to quiz her further. He would find out. In time.

'We want you to start on Monday,' he said instead, watching her expression closely. 'Is that too soon for you? Or have you changed your mind about joining us?'

She was quiet for a few moments. 'Monday's fine.' She slid a glance in his direction. 'And I wouldn't have applied for the job, far less come here for the night, if I had any intention of changing my mind about accepting it.'

She didn't sound convinced.

'Will it be a problem us working together?' he said. It was the only reason he could think of for her hesitation.

'Now, why would you think that?' she said lightly. 'We had a brief—er—thing months ago. Hardly a reason to avoid one another.'

'Was that all it was, Cassie? A thing? I could have sworn there was more.'

He thought he saw a flash of pain in her eyes, but then she smiled sadly. 'It was good, really good, and I don't regret a moment of it, but neither of us were looking for something permanent, were we?'

What could he say to that? That he had thought that there could be something, and he'd been sure she had felt the same? But he'd been wrong and she was right. What was the point in raking over something that had happened so many months ago?

Cassie shivered. 'I think I'll go back to my room now.'

He pulled his sweater off and, ignoring her protests, tugged it over her head, amused to see it reached to well below her knees.

She looked him directly in the eyes and for a second he saw something flare in their depths. And he knew then that whatever she said, whatever had been between them, had never truly gone. For either of them.

CHAPTER FIVE

CASSIE PERCHED ON the edge of her chair, holding onto her mug of coffee as if it were a life jacket and she was about to be tossed into a stormy sea. She took a deep, surreptitious breath and forced herself to relax. Today would be the first time she'd be seeing patients since Afghanistan. Although she felt anxious, her longing to get back to work was greater. Everyone was smiling at her, doing their best to make her feel welcome—Jenny, the receptionist, and the nurses, Vicki and Julie.

Even the cleaner, a stout lady called Gladys, had been introduced earlier. 'Keep on the right side of Gladys,' Rose had whispered, 'and she'll see you right. She's been here since Jonathan's uncle's time and will probably see us all out.'

'Now you've met everyone,' Jonathan said when they were all gathered in the elegant, high-ceilinged staff meeting room, 'let's discuss what we have on.'

'We have six coming in to see Vicki, the same number to see Julie, around a dozen over the course of the day on Jonathan and Leith's clinics, and I've taken the liberty of booking in a couple of new patients for you, Cassie, as well as the drop-ins, if that's okay?' Rose said.

'The more the better,' Cassie replied.

'Don't worry, we'll have you working at full pelt in no time at all. It's just that our regulars like to see their usual doctors if at all possible.' She turned to Leith. 'Speaking of which, the Duchess of Fotheringham is coming incognito for her antenatal visit with you, Leith. I've put her at the end of the list when most of the others have left. Apart from that we have a request from her that you and another doctor go to their Caribbean island next month with them as part of their house party. That would be for a few days. They wanted Fabio but as he's not available, could I put you down for that trip, Cassie?'

Cassie's head jerked up. She glanced over at Leith, who was looking at her with his head cocked to one side and a small smile on his face.

She wished the other doctor could be anyone but him. She wasn't quite ready to spend time with him outside work, but she could hardly refuse to go.

'Sure,' she said. 'That would be fine. But does she really need a paediatrician?'

'The Duchess was born prematurely and her mother had a couple of miscarriages before her, so she's understandably a little anxious,' Leith said. 'She'll be thirty weeks at the time of the trip and as their home on the Caribbean is a little way from a major hospital, she's asked for both a paediatrician and an obstetrician to accompany her. It's only for a week and, of course, if I had any high-risk pregnancies that were due to deliver around that time, I would have had to say no.' He shrugged. 'But as I don't...'

Cassie wondered again if she'd made a mistake, taking this job. It all sounded very different from the work she'd been doing in Afghanistan and Sudan. Would she cope with looking after patients who weren't really ill, just demanding?

She quickly realised that not all her patients were coming to see her with colds and vague aches and pains. Her second patient was a teenage girl with swollen glands who Cassie thought might have glandular fever. Not sure how to go about ordering more tests, she went in search of advice. As luck would have it, the first person she came across was Leith, who was chatting with Jenny about fitting in a patient as an emergency.

He explained who she needed to call to rush the results, but despite his usual politeness he seemed distracted—almost offhand.

It was on the tip of Cassie's tongue to ask him if something was wrong but she bit back the words. Hadn't she promised herself that she wouldn't let herself become involved in his life? She had to keep their relationship on a professional footing.

As soon as she'd taken blood from the teenager and advised her to go home to rest, Cassie went back to Reception to find out whether there was anything else she could do. She'd go stir crazy if she wasn't kept busy.

The waiting room was half-full, but when she checked the diary, none of the patients were scheduled to see her. Jenny was on the phone, looking excited.

As she was about to turn away, the receptionist signalled to her to wait. 'That was Fabio on
the phone. Katie is having some mild contractions so he's asking if you would cover for him.
He says to call him if you have any questions.
Or to ask Leith.'

Leith was at the desk, filling out some blood-
test forms. He glanced up. 'Just yell if you need
me.'

'Sure,' Cassie replied, glad that she would have
something to do that didn't involve studying her
fingertips.

'If you could take Mrs Mohammed there? The
lady with the young girl? That would be a help.'

Mrs Mohammed was an anxious-looking
woman holding a child of around three in her
lap. The little girl clung to her mother, darting
anxious glances in Cassie's direction. Cassie
crossed over to them.

'I'm Dr Ross,' she introduced herself. 'Would
you like to come through to my consulting
room?'

'No!' the little girl cried. 'Not going! Take me
home, Mummy. Want to go now!'

'Come now, darling, the doctor's not going to hurt you. She wants to make you better.'

But the child wrapped her arms around her mother's neck and hung on even more tightly.

'Jasmine's your name, isn't it?' Cassie asked. 'It's a pretty name.'

The little girl released her hold on her mother's neck and regarded Cassie with steady brown eyes. 'My mummy's called Imani. That's a pretty name too.'

'Yes, it is. And my name's Cassie.'

'Are you a doctor?'

'Yes. But not a scary one.'

'Don't like doctors.'

'It's okay, Jasmine,' Cassie said gently. 'I'm not going to hurt you, but I need to look in your throat and listen to your chest.'

Jasmine shook her head before burying her face in her mother's chest.

'Tell you what, Jasmine, why don't I listen to Teddy's chest first?' She picked up a teddy from the pile of toys next to the chair. 'He's not been feeling very well either, and I need you to help me find out why not.'

The child slowly released her grip on her

mother and turned to look at the teddy. Cassie made a big show of listening to his chest and nodding. 'Mmm. Nothing a day in bed won't cure, and possibly some ice cream might help too, if his throat his sore,' she said. 'Would you like to listen through my special hearing thing?'

When Jasmine nodded, Cassie placed the stethoscope in the girl's ears and let her listen to Teddy's chest. Then Jasmine listened to her mother's chest too.

'Now, can I listen to yours?' Cassie said before Jasmine asked to listen to hers. 'We can stay here, but it would be better to do it in my room.' She held out her hand. 'Would you bring Teddy for me?'

The little girl thought about it for a few moments before making up her mind. She slid from her mother's lap and, still holding Teddy, held out her hand to Cassie.

As they passed the reception desk on their way to Cassie's room, Leith, out of sight of the mother, smiled at Cassie. 'Good job,' he murmured.

Jasmine, having decided to trust Cassie, allowed herself to be examined—as long as Teddy was subjected to the same treatment. As Cassie had suspected, she had little wrong with her that a couple of days in bed wouldn't put right.

But when her relieved mother stood up, she cried out in pain and pressed her hands to her abdomen.

'What is it?' Cassie asked.

'Mummy's tummy sore,' Jasmine said. 'Mummy's tummy sore *a lot.*'

'Is that right?'

Imani shook her head dismissively. 'It's nothing. It comes and goes. It's not too bad.'

'Jasmine, would you wait outside with one of the nurses while I talk to your mummy?'

When Jasmine shook her head and stuck her thumb in her mouth, Cassie knew there was no chance of separating the child from her mother.

'Jasmine, could you go to the window and show Teddy the garden?' Cassie requested, and to her relief the little girl did as she was asked, talking to the soft toy as she pointed out different birds in the garden.

While Jasmine was occupied, Cassie took a brief history from her mother. Apart from this pain, which had started a few months ago, she wasn't on any medication and didn't have any other symptoms.

'Is it okay if Jasmine stays while I examine you? I just want to feel your abdomen.'

Imani nodded.

When Imani was settled on the examination couch, Cassie palpated her abdomen. There was definitely something there that shouldn't be.

'I think it would be useful for Dr Ballantyne to see you. He's the practice gynaecologist/obstetrician and I think he'd have a better idea about what's causing you pain than I do.'

Imani shook her head. 'I don't wish to see a male doctor.'

Cassie lowered her voice. 'Then I should refer you to hospital. You can see a female obstetrician there.'

'Really, no thank you. It is nothing. So much fuss for nothing.'

But Cassie knew it wasn't nothing.

'Would you object to my having a quick talk with Dr Ballantyne while you wait?'

'If you must.'

Cassie left her, and after checking that Leith had no one with him knocked on his consulting-room door. When he saw it was her, he gave a distracted smile. As his green eyes locked onto hers, her heart did an annoying hippity-hop and she had to force herself not to look away.

'Cassie! Something up?'

'I need advice.' Quickly she outlined everything Imani had told her. 'Naturally I took a full history. The only thing of note is that she's experiencing intermittent pain in her lower abdomen. On examination I felt something—but I'm not sure what. I plan to do a full blood screen, of course.'

Leith was immediately on his feet. 'You want me to see her?'

'Ideally yes, but she won't hear of it.'

'Why not?'

'I'm not sure. I suspect she only wants to be examined by a female doctor.'

'I see.' He sat back down and narrowed his eyes as he thought. It was the same thing he'd always done when he was concentrating, whether on patients—or on her.

As the memory of how thoroughly he'd concentrated on her on those last days on the Mercy

Ship, heat rushed to her cheeks. Cassie forced the image away.

'Nothing's likely to change in the next twenty-four hours,' Leith said after a moment. 'In addition to the bloods, I suggest you do a pelvic scan—ask if she'll allow Vicki to help you. Once we have the results we can speak again.'

He swivelled his chair so that his back was towards her and started drumming his pen on his knee. There was something about the set of his shoulders that bothered her.

'Is everything all right?' she asked.

He was silent for so long she wondered if he'd even heard her question.

'I'm expecting a call from my solicitor this afternoon,' he said finally, his mouth set in a grim line. 'About Peter and whether I'm going to be granted greater access rights or—even better—shared custody. The decision will be made later today.'

Before she realised what she was doing she had crossed the room and taken his hand. 'I hope everything works out, Leith. I'm sure you'll make a good dad.'

She caught her breath as he looked deep into

her eyes. He squeezed her fingers briefly before letting go. 'I'm going to do my best for my son. He deserves that.'

After she'd finished seeing to Imani, who had reluctantly promised to return in a couple of days to get the results of the tests, Cassie was kept busy for the rest of the afternoon with a number of patients who had dropped in unexpectedly.

When she'd seen everyone, she went to the staff kitchen to make herself a cup of coffee. Rose was there before her. 'How's it going?' she asked. 'Settling in?'

'It's busier than I thought,' Cassie admitted. 'But I like that.'

'We try to keep the afternoons free for drop-ins or home visits,' Rose said, filling their mugs with hot water from the kettle. 'Organising the day can take a lot of juggling—particularly when we're asked to accompany patients abroad.'

'It must be difficult. I have to say I didn't expect to have my first trip scheduled so quickly. Not that I'm complaining,' she added quickly. 'Who wouldn't want to visit the Caribbean?'

'Jonathan and I can't really do trips any longer

because of Daisy—or at least I can't, although Jonathan has to when no one else is available or when a patient asks for him particularly. Fabio obviously doesn't want to travel right now, so I'm afraid you and Leith will be our first port of call if we get any more requests. Of course, if Leith gets shared custody of his son he'll be more restricted too.

'We really need more doctors and nurses on a permanent basis. The practice is growing so fast it's hard to keep up. Jonathan would prefer to keep it small, but unless he starts turning patients away we're going to have no choice but to take on more staff.' She eyed Cassie speculatively. 'Do you like living in London? Could you see yourself back here permanently?'

'I do like London, but I'm not ready to put down roots. Sometimes I wonder if I ever will,' Cassie replied, taking her mug from Rose.

'No one special then?' Rose asked, tipping her head to one side. 'I would have thought someone like you would have them queuing up at the door.'

Cassie grimaced. 'I really don't do the whole

relationship thing. I like my independence too much to give it up.'

Rose raised an eyebrow. 'Marriage doesn't necessarily mean giving up your independence. Quite the opposite.' She smiled dreamily.

Cassie looked at her askance. In her book there was nothing to recommend marriage. As far as she knew, her biological father had abandoned her mother the second he'd found out she was pregnant and, as far as she could tell, her adoptive parents had only stayed together because of appearances—the same reason they had adopted a child whom they'd never been able to love.

She remembered the day she'd found out that the Rosses were not her real parents.

She hadn't been able to sleep so she'd got out of bed, intending to go downstairs and ask her mother for a glass of milk.

But when she'd got to the top of the stairs she'd heard her parents talking in angry voices. So she'd sat down and listened.

'I don't think I can continue like this,' Mummy had been saying. 'I simply can't manage her.'

Cassie hadn't been able to hear what her father

had said in reply. He always spoke more softly than her mother.

'I don't care what the social workers say. I won't have a child in this house that won't do as she's told. Cassie will find new parents, I'm sure. A couple who are more suited to deal with a child with her needs.'

Cassie was puzzled. What needs? She didn't want new parents. What could they mean?

'Give her time, Lily. At least she's well be-haved. A little stubborn perhaps, but she's a pretty child and any tendency to her becoming like her birth mother can be moulded out of her.'

Cassie's heart felt like it was about to explode. She didn't know what a birth mother was, but suddenly the memory of a woman she'd once called Mummy too—a different mummy, one who was loving most times except when she was sick—rushed back into her head. But that mummy had sent her away. And now it seemed her new mummy wanted to do the same. She ran back to her bed and hid under the covers. Was there a place naughty children were sent? Was it hell? She shivered all through the night, but at the end of it she resolved to be as good as gold. So good that she would never get sent away. Again. Nanny arrived soon after that day.

'Are you all right?' Rose's voice pulled her back to the present.

Cassie forced a smile. 'I'm fine.'

'Are you sure? You looked so sad there for a moment,' Rose persisted.

'Now, what would I have to be sad about?' she replied lightly. 'I have everything anyone could ever want.'

Leith tossed his pen onto the table and slumped back in his chair. Perhaps he should have gone home to wait for the call, but he would have driven himself crazy without something to distract him. Besides, with Fabio on alert in case the Braxton-Hicks contractions Katie was having turned into full-blown labour, the practice was even more short-staffed than usual.

The court battle had been an excruciating process with brief flurries of activity followed by long delays as his solicitors waited for reports from what seemed to be hundreds of different professionals—half of whom seemed to be on holiday exactly when they were needed. But none of that would matter as long as he got decent access to his son.

At times he'd wondered if he was doing the right thing to persist with the court case. Had Cassie been right? Was it fair to uproot a child from everything he knew? But he didn't think like that for long. Perhaps if Jude had been a better mother he would have left things the way they were. Peter had the right to know his father. To know that there was someone in his life who would move heaven and hell to be with him.

Just when he thought he could stand the suspense no longer, the phone rang. He snatched at it. He listened for a few minutes then sank back down on the chair. It was over. Or almost.

CHAPTER SIX

'I THINK YOU should let Leith have a look at these,' Jonathan said to Cassie a few days later, handing her Imani's notes. The results of the blood tests had been normal but the pelvic scan was a different story. Sure enough, there was something on one of her ovaries that didn't look normal. Frustratingly, Imani still refused to let Cassie refer her to hospital.

'I would if Leith was here,' Cassie said.

'Damn, I'd forgotten he isn't coming in today. He has his son for the first time, doesn't he?'

'So I understand.'

The staff at the practice had been buzzing with the news that, finally, although he hadn't won sole custody, he had been awarded regular access to Peter, including weekends and school holidays. Today was to be the first day father and son would meet without either Jude's mother or sister being present. Cassie wondered how it was going.

'I think you should pop over to his flat and show him her notes.' Jonathan handed back the results.

'I don't think it's fair to disrupt his day,' Cassie protested.

'I'm sure he won't mind. His flat is only a short distance from here. Let me check if he's in.' Before Cassie could protest, Jonathan had lifted the phone and was dialling. 'Do you have anyone waiting to see you?' he asked Cassie as he waited for his call to be answered.

Cassie shook her head. But she didn't want to meet up with Leith—especially not when he was with Peter. It was difficult enough working alongside him.

To her dismay, judging by the side of the conversation she could hear, it seemed as if she was going to have to do just that.

'He's at home. Apparently he tried to get Peter to go to the park but he didn't want to. To be honest, he sounded relieved to have an interruption.'

That didn't bode too well.

A short while later, Cassie found herself outside the door of a smart Edwardian tenement.

And, sure enough, as Jonathan suspected, Leith looked relieved to see her.

'Come in, Cassie.'

'I'm not staying. Jonathan thought I should bring you Imani's results to look at.' She passed him the paper.

'At least come and say hello to Peter while I have a look.' He didn't just sound relieved, he sounded desperate.

Cassie followed him down a long corridor with a highly polished floor into an open-plan sitting room, dining room and kitchen, furnished in heavy dark wood and leather, warmed by bright rugs, cushions and bookshelves crammed with books. Colourful abstract paintings hung alongside or above African masks and artefacts. Not quite the minimalist bachelor pad she'd imagined but a lived-in home that, she realised, reflected what she knew of Leith.

The little boy was sitting on the edge of a leather sofa, ignoring the cartoon on the widescreen TV and instead staring blankly at the floor. His olive complexion must have been inherited from his mother, although he had Leith's unusual green eyes and light brown hair. It was a striking combination.

'Peter, this is one of my colleagues, Dr Ross,' Leith said.

The boy slid his eyes towards them and then returned to staring at the floor.

But in that short glance Cassie saw again the same lost and lonely look she'd seen in his photo, and her heart ached for him. She went to sit next to him.

'Hello, Peter. You can call me Cassie, if you like.'

There was no reaction from the little boy.

Leith rubbed a hand across his face. 'Say hello, Peter.' He looked at Cassie. 'He hasn't said a word since he arrived, except "no". I tried to give him a snack but he wouldn't take it. He doesn't want to go to the park or to the library.'

The library! It wasn't the first place she would have thought of taking a little boy of six. She noticed Peter had a soft toy gripped in his fingers.

'Who's that you have there?' she asked softly.

'Mr Mouse.' The words were softly spoken. Still, he didn't look at her.

'And is Mr Mouse feeling okay?' Cassie asked.

'He doesn't like it here.'

'Now, why can that be? Is he a bit scared because everything is different? Or is he missing his mummy?'

'He's worried about *my* mummy. He knows she doesn't like being on her own.'

Leith seemed utterly bewildered.

'Well, she won't be alone for long, will she? Not when she has your aunty and your gran to keep her company,' Leith said.

'Mummy likes *me* to keep her company,' Peter replied sullenly.

'I can see why your mummy would like to have you to keep her company,' Cassie said.

This time, Peter did look up. 'I make her tea,' he said proudly. 'She says I'm big enough to be the man of the house.' He flicked his eyes towards Leith. 'We don't need him. Mummy says he wants to take me away from her.'

The look of bewilderment on Leith's face changed to one of fury and Cassie shook her head in warning. Now was not the time to challenge Jude's obvious manipulation of her son.

'I'm sure your mummy loves you very much,

but so does your daddy. That's why he wants to spend time with you. He doesn't want to take you away from your mummy. He just wants to share you.'

'I don't want to be shared.' Peter hugged Mr Mouse tighter.

Cassie held out her hand. 'I can see you're not interested in watching television. Why don't you, me and Daddy go to the park for a little while? I passed it on the way here and it has all sorts of fun things in it. Perhaps we can all get a burger after? What do you say?'

Peter studied her for a long moment. 'I'll go if you go,' he said finally.

Cassie smiled. 'Didn't I just say I would? Now, I need to speak to your daddy about something very quickly. Then we'll go.'

When she stood up, Leith indicated with his head that she should follow him into the kitchen. It looked as if a tornado had hit it. There were dishes piled in the sink and pink milk spilled on the black granite countertop.

'What happened here?' she asked.

'I tried to make him a milkshake. Seems like I forgot to put the lid of the blender on. Took me half an hour to hunt the damn thing down in the first place. In the end I only managed to make enough for half a glass. He wouldn't even take a sip.'

Cassie hid a smile. 'Give him time, Leith. Think of it from his point of view. He barely knows you and from what you told me on the ship—and from what he's saying—his mother has him very confused.'

'How dare she tell him that I want to take him from her?' A muscle in his jaw twitched. 'I'm more sure than ever she's not fit to look after him.'

'Perhaps she fears losing him to you? But Peter loves her, Leith. She must be doing something right.'

'I don't want good-enough-some-of-the-time for my son.'

Cassie flinched inwardly.

'Of course you don't,' she replied. *Which is why I can never be a part of your life—and Peter's,* she finished silently, aware of the familiar ache lodging itself in her chest.

Leith picked up the notes Cassie had brought and flicked through them.

'Remind me about this lady. She's a previously fit and healthy twenty-five-year-old with recent onset of abdominal pain and on examination you felt a mass?'

'Correct.'

'And if I remember correctly, she reported that the lower abdominal pain she was experiencing intermittently would go away on its own after a few hours. So you decided to do a pelvic scan.'

'It was you who suggested it. All the routine bloods are normal but the scan shows an abnormality. I'm not sure what I'm seeing, so Jonathan suggested I bring it to you to have a look.'

Leith studied the pelvic scan. 'These images almost certainly show a dermoid cyst.'

'And the prognosis?'

'Not good generally but we may have caught her in the earliest stages of the illness. She'll have to have the cyst removed first—hopefully without having to remove the ovary at the same time.'

Poor Imani. Although Cassie had no intention of having children, she knew most women were devastated when the option was taken away from them. 'As long as she has one ovary, she'll still be able to have more children.'

'But if we don't get to the primary cause, her condition will get worse. Do you have her mobile number?'

'No, but it should be on her notes. I'll give her a ring right now, shall I?'

By the time Cassie had called Imani and persuaded her to come in the next morning, Peter was waiting at the door.

'Is it time for me to go home now?' he asked hopefully.

'No, sweetie. We're going to go to the park first, remember? Your daddy will take you back to your gran's after that.'

Peter slipped his hand into hers. 'You'll stay till then?'

Over the top of Peter's head Cassie caught Leith's eyes and she saw the desperation in them. Then she knew. Like it or not, it was too late to back out now. She was already involved with Leith and his son.

CHAPTER SEVEN

CASSIE FINISHED WRITING her notes and leaned back in her chair. Leith had been correct in his diagnosis. He'd removed the cyst and Imani was home once again and recovering. It had been a good call. There was a knock on the door and without waiting for an invitation to enter, Leith strode in.

It had been a couple of weeks since she'd gone to his flat and since then she'd been with Leith and Peter to the movies and on the London Eye on both Saturdays—Leith's usual access day. The little boy still barely acknowledged his father, but he was beginning to relax with Cassie. However, if she tried to leave him alone with his father, Peter would panic and grab her.

'I need to speak to you,' Leith said. His usual calm, easygoing manner was absent. Instead, he looked like someone near the end of his tether.

'Okay,' Cassie replied calmly. 'Coffee?'

Leith shook his head. 'I need you to come to Skye with me for a few days. Can you do it?'

Cassie frowned. 'A patient?'

'No. Nothing like that,' Leith replied. 'I have Peter for the whole long weekend and I want to take him to meet his grandparents. I need you to come with me.'

'Why me?' Cassie asked after a long pause.

'I doubt Peter will be happy to spend four days with me unless you're there.' He paused. 'Please, Cassie. I just don't know how to win him over.' He pulled a hand across his face. 'It will be easier for him to have you there. You've seen how he is with me.'

'He'll warm to you eventually. Give him time.'

'Eventually isn't soon enough, Cassie. Right now it's you he feels comfortable with. He trusts you. You have a way with children. They're instinctively drawn to you. It doesn't matter where in the world they are. Here. Africa. Remember Maria's little boy? You couldn't even speak his language, yet it didn't matter.'

As soon as he mentioned Africa, Cassie was back there. She could almost hear the cicadas, smell the sea, feel Leith's arms around her, his lips on hers.

She shook her head in an attempt to clear it. What were they talking about? Oh, yes, some crazy suggestion that she go with him and Peter to Skye.

It was impossible. Go away with Leith? To his family home? When she'd promised herself she would keep her distance as much as possible?

So why then had she spent those couple of days with Peter and Leith? Now, see what it had started. But that was different. That was a matter of a few hours, not days.

An image of the timid little boy flashed into her head and she tried to push it away.

'Do you think it's fair to take him away at this stage?' she said.

Leith's face darkened. 'Do you have any idea how long I've fought for this? Finally I have the moral—and legal—right to be with him and I need—want—to spend time with him. I want him to meet my parents and I know he'll love Skye once he gets there. It's a wonderful place for children.'

'Put yourself in his shoes,' Cassie said gently. 'As you say, he doesn't really know you yet. Skye will seem a very strange and alien place to him—and you'll be introducing him to more strange people.'

'I realise that,' Leith admitted. 'But it's the first time I have access for the whole weekend and if I don't take him to Skye I don't know how the two of us would manage on our own.' He looked so anguished that Cassie's heart went out to him. 'Maybe I am expecting too much too soon,' Leith continued after a moment. 'God, Cassie, do you have any idea how it feels to have your child look at you as if you were some sort of monster?'

'You love him. In the end that's all that really matters. He'll come to believe that in time.'

'I'm not giving up until he does. So, will you come? I need you as a buffer—just until he comes to trust me.'

He seemed so woebegone, she felt herself melt. He was so competent in every other area of his life yet a six-year-old had him beaten. 'I don't know, Leith. Isn't there anyone else you could ask?'

'It's you he wants. You're the only one familiar to him. And, as you just said, more strangers aren't what he needs right now.'

Damn! Hoisted by her own petard! 'But the whole weekend, Leith? Can the practice do without us both?' She knew as she said the words that she was caving in.

'We'll leave on Saturday morning. It's a public holiday on Monday and Tuesday, remember? There's only ever one of us on call at a time and it's scheduled to be Jonathan's turn. We'll fly to Glasgow or Inverness and drive from there' His expression cleared. 'We'll be back by Tuesday evening.'

She still wanted to say no—she really didn't want to spend time with Leith or get more involved in his life—but how could she refuse? It wasn't as if she had anything lined up for the weekend. And it wasn't Leith she'd be doing it for—it was Peter.

'Okay, you've convinced me,' she said. 'I'll do it this once, but after that you're on your own. Agreed?'

He grinned at her and it was as if all the tiny hairs on the back of her neck were standing to attention. 'Thanks, Cassie. I owe you.'

* * *

The next day, Cassie was asked to see a child in his home.

The address of her patient was in Kensington and Cassie found herself outside a grand Edwardian town house.

Wealth and a title didn't stop you from having a sick child, she thought as she ran up the steps. But surely it made things easier? However, in Cassie's experience, rich or poor, the mothers— and fathers—with a sick child were all the same. Scared and worried.

From the notes she'd read she didn't think the girl she was to see was ill—at least, not physically. It sounded as if she was a little slow with her development markers, but Cassie had met enough anxious parents to know that they often grossly over-estimated where their child should be.

The door was opened by the housekeeper. Cassie hid a smile. Really, did people still live like that in this day and age? 'Madam will be with you shortly,' the housekeeper said. 'If you could wait here?' She pointed to a chair in the large reception hall.

After ten minutes Cassie was getting irritated. Even if she was being paid for her services it really was unforgivably rude of Mrs Forsythe to keep her waiting like this. However, it was possible she was with her daughter and of course Cassie wouldn't want her to rush her.

More time passed and, frustrated, she got to her feet. She'd already studied every portrait and painting that adorned the walls and she should get back to the practice.

She decided to have a peek into the rooms that led off the hall to see if she could find the missing mother. The first room on the left was an enormous dining room, set with sparkling crystal and fine china, as if Mrs Forsythe was expecting guests for lunch at any moment.

The room next door was equally grand with its high ceiling and ornate cornicing. The brilliant white linen upholstery looked elegant but uninviting. It was a lovely room, but Cassie wouldn't describe it as homely or welcoming.

But it was the last door she opened that shocked Cassie. At first she thought she'd stumbled into a storage room, but then at the opposite end of the room she noticed a playpen.

The room was probably where Mrs Forsythe kept her daughter's toys and equipment out of sight when she was expecting guests. It would save carting it all back up to the playroom, which she guessed would be on one of the upper floors.

Just as she was about to turn away a sound startled her. There in the playpen was a girl of around three, standing gripping the edge of the playpen and watching Cassie with large mournful eyes. This had to be Letitia.

What was the child doing here on her own? Perhaps the mother had left her sleeping? Or had a baby monitor in the room where Cassie couldn't see it?

Nevertheless, Cassie had an uneasy feeling. A child of this age shouldn't be left in a playpen.

'Hello,' she said quietly.

There was no response.

'What's your name?' Cassie tried again. The child continued to look at her with blank eyes. Then the little girl sat down and, thumb in her mouth, opened a book and began to flick through the pages. At least she wasn't without stimulation altogether.

'Oh, you must forgive me for keeping you.' The

voice came from the door and Cassie whirled round to find a woman, skinny almost to the point of gauntness, in the doorway. 'Has Letitia been keeping you company?'

It seemed an odd thing to say.

'Is it Letitia who I've come to see?' Cassie asked.

'Yes.'

Cassie noticed that Mrs Forsythe had made no move towards her daughter or even looked in her direction. There really was something odd going on here.

'And what seems to be the matter?'

'You can see for yourself. She doesn't seem to take any real interest in what's going on around her.'

Cassie was beginning to suspect where the problem lay.

'Perhaps you could lift Letitia out of the play-pen?' she suggested, 'so I can have a look at her.'

Mrs Forsythe lifted her daughter up but it was clear that it wasn't something she was comfortable doing.

'I did have a nanny to help in the beginning,' Mrs Forsythe said, 'until Letitia was six months old. But then she left and I haven't quite managed to sort anyone else out. My husband isn't really keen on my hiring a new nanny. He says I should look after Letitia myself. He was brought up by nannies and hated it. But, frankly, I don't see how he can expect me to be with Letitia all day.' She lowered her voice. 'It's so boring. It's not as if I can take her with me to lunch or to the gym.'

Cassie was horrified. This woman was talking about her daughter as if she were an unwanted Christmas present.

She gritted her teeth and, ignoring the impatient glances Mrs Forsythe was giving her watch, examined the child.

'I'd like you to bring her down to the practice for some more tests,' she said eventually, striving to keep her voice matter-of–fact, although inside she was seething.

She was pretty certain that all that was wrong with Letitia was lack of stimulation and parental attention. Why did some women have children when it was clear that they were not cut out for motherhood? Was the stigma against childless women still so strong? She was certain it was the only reason Lily had adopted her, but surely times had changed?

'Could you bring Letitia in tomorrow?' She wasn't even sure why she was suggesting it, but she wanted the opportunity to discuss the little girl with her colleagues—perhaps even have Fabio come in to assess her. She needed to be certain her own prejudices weren't clouding her judgement.

'I'm not sure about tomorrow,' Mrs Forsythe said. 'Is it really urgent?'

'It's not life-threatening, no. But I would like to see her again as soon as possible so I can carry out some more tests.'

Mrs Forsythe looked thoughtful. 'I suppose I might be able to bring her in next week. I'll have to check my diary first, though.'

'Oh, for heaven's sake, Mrs Forsythe.' Cassie couldn't help it any more. This woman had no right to call herself a mother. 'Nothing—I repeat, nothing—is more important than the welfare of your child. Why the hell did you have her if you can't be bothered with her?' It was as if all the years of frustration had built up inside her and was going to erupt. She had to get out of here before she really told this woman exactly what she thought of her.

Mrs Forsythe paled. 'Well,' she said, 'I really don't think there's any need...'

But Cassie wasn't listening. She closed her medical bag with a snap and before Mrs Forsythe could say any more, she let herself out of the house.

She was still breathing deeply when she arrived back at Harley Street. All she wanted was to get to the privacy of her consulting room before anyone noticed her agitation.

But to her dismay the first person she bumped into was Leith.

He tipped his head at her. 'Walked it off yet?'

'And what is that supposed to mean?' she demanded.

Leith took her by the arm and led her into his room. 'Mrs Forsythe has been on the phone. What on earth did you say to upset her? She's refusing to bring her child to see you. Says you were unforgivably rude and unprofessional.'

'*I* was rude?'

'Why don't you tell me about it?' Leith said calmly.

'The woman is a monster. She keeps her child isolated in a playpen because she can't be bothered with her. She wonders why her little girl seems to be slower than her friends' children and can't seem to understand that it's probably to do with the lack of stimulation and love from her mother.'

Cassie was pacing up and down. The tension was continuing to build inside her and she knew she should take some time out to get herself back together but somehow now that she'd started she couldn't stop. 'I'll never understand why some women have children. There should be a test.'

Leith said nothing, just raised one eyebrow.

'Mrs Forsythe has everything money can buy and access to all the help she needs, yet, as a mother, she's not a patch on those women we saw in Africa.'

'Have you considered the possibility that she's depressed?' Leith asked.

'That woman is no more depressed than I am!'

'Are you sure?' He sat down and hooked his arms behind his head. 'Cassie, what's going on? You must have come across women like Mrs Forsythe before!'

All of a sudden the fury leaked away and Cassie was horrified. What on earth had all that been about? Leith was right. She *had* come across women like Mrs Forsythe before—not often but a few times in her career—and she'd never reacted like this. It had been completely and utterly unprofessional. For the first time she could ever remember she had lost her professional objectivity—something she prided herself on. She sank down in the chair opposite Leith.

'My God,' she whispered. Using every ounce of self-control in her, she forced herself to breathe deeply. 'I've never reacted that way before.'

'It happens to most of us at some time,' Leith said. Cassie doubted that. 'Luckily, I was the one who took her call and I think I managed to persuade her to come in and see Fabio. But she might still complain to Jonathan, I'm afraid. Not that Jonathan will necessarily believe everything she says, but this practice takes patient complaints very seriously.'

Cassie closed her eyes. She had never, ever had anyone complain about her and yet here she was less than three weeks into a job and she had upset a patient.

'What makes it worse,' she said, 'was that Letitia might be the one to suffer from my conduct. Her mother might decide not to seek any further professional help at all.'

'I think you should go to Jonathan and let him know what happened.'

Cassie stumbled to her feet, bright red with mortification. 'Of course,' she said. 'I'll go now.'

To her surprise, Jonathan wasn't annoyed in the slightest.

'I doubt I would have reacted very differently,' he said. 'But…' he held up a finger '…we cannot let personal feelings get in the way of doing the right thing by our patients. And it is Letitia who is our patient, not the mother.'

Cassie sank down into the armchair. 'I know. I'm sorry. I really don't know what got into me.' But Jonathan deserved more than that.

'I…' She licked her lips. 'I was brought up by a woman—my adoptive mother—who couldn't bear the sight of me. I'm sorry…little Letitia brought it all back. And I've not been the same since…'

Jonathan leant forward and studied her intently. 'Since?'

But she couldn't bring herself to continue. She was too afraid she'd break down and it was all too humiliating as it was. She stumbled to her feet. 'I let my own experiences cloud my judgement. I'm sorry. It won't happen again.' And leaving an astonished Jonathan staring after her, she made her exit with what little dignity she had left.

Later that afternoon there was a soft tap on the door and Rose popped her head in.

'Are you free for a coffee?' she asked.

Without waiting for a reply, Rose pushed the door open with her hip and placed a mug down on the desk.

'Black, isn't it?'

Cassie nodded. She had a good idea what had brought Rose to her office and she didn't know how she felt about it. Embarrassed? Certainly. And also anxious. She had apologised and Jonathan had seemed to accept her apology with good grace. But what if they decided that she wasn't a good fit for their practice? All these years she had managed to present a cool, unruffled façade to everyone, yet she'd barely been here a month and she'd allowed her guard to slip in the most unprofessional way possible.

She took a sip of coffee before placing it back down on the table.

'It's okay,' she said to Rose, 'if you want to let me go. I perfectly understand.'

Rose's eyes widened. 'Whatever do you mean?'

'If you and Jonathan have decided that I'm not a good match for the practice because of what happened with Mrs Forsythe…'

'Goodness me, Cassie,' Rose said with a laugh. 'Whatever must you think of us? There isn't one of us who hasn't had a moment with a patient and had to rely on one of the other staff to smooth things over. And for the record, I've never liked Mrs Forsythe anyway. She's one of those women who think that we should drop whatever we're doing to run and see her every time she has a sniffle. Not even our richest or most influential patients expect that—except perhaps for the sheikh. If it wasn't for little Letitia we would have taken Mrs Forsythe off our list months ago.

'No, it was you Jonathan was worried about.' She set her own mug down and leaned back in the chair. 'He had a pretty cold and unloving upbringing too. He only told me what you told him because he wanted to make sure you were all right.'

Rose leaned over and took Cassie's hand. 'We like to think of everyone in this practice as part of our family—and that means accepting there will be differences of opinion, even the occasional fallout. We all make mistakes, but in the end we all have to support each other. Do you understand?'

There was a lump in Cassie's throat the size of a golf ball. She didn't know if she could speak so she simply nodded.

'Is there anything you'd like to talk about?' Rose asked. 'I'm good at keeping things to myself.'

There was genuine concern in her voice and Cassie smiled, remembering that Leith had said the same thing. 'No, really. I'm okay now. But thanks.'

'I won't probe,' Rose said, getting to her feet, 'but if you ever need to chat, I'm your woman.

Wild horses—or even Gladys—won't drag your secrets from me.'

When the door closed behind Rose, Cassie felt touched. These people hardly knew her and she'd acted in a way that could have brought their practice into disrepute, yet all their concern was for her.

Some of the tightness in her chest eased. For once she hadn't been perfect, yet no one had turned away.

Leith pushed away from his desk.

He couldn't concentrate. Every time he tried to write a report his mind kept wandering back to Cassie.

It was strange seeing her every day. Strange but good. He found himself looking out for her, smiling when he caught glimpses of her as she went about her work. The same way he had constantly looked out for her on the Mercy Ship.

Everything about her reminded him of their time in Africa. He just had to catch sight of her and he was transported back there to the feel of her in his arms, the way she'd laughed up at him, the way his heart had lifted, still lifted, when-ever he saw her.

He picked up his pen then threw it back down. It was no use. Who was he trying to kid? The last weeks had shown him that his feelings for her weren't in the past. They were still there. Deeper than ever.

But he still didn't have a clue what was going on under that calm, distant exterior she liked to show the world—the world with the exception of Peter. She was different with him. Funny, teas-ing, affectionate. If he was honest with himself, he envied her for her natural way with Peter—something he was still trying to emulate and was failing miserably at.

It was a cop-out to ask her to go with him. Surely he should be able to manage his son by himself by now? But Peter still made it clear he hated being with him—yet he had formed an attachment to Cassie and she hadn't even ap-peared to be trying.

She was the same with Peter as she was with all her patients, relentlessly kind, patient, caring. He hadn't been wrong about that side of her, so perhaps he hadn't been wrong at all?

So what had that issue with Mrs Forsythe been about? He'd never seen Cassie lose her cool, not even when confronted with the most testing situations on board the ship, and there had been plenty of them.

He was more certain than ever that she was keeping something from him. What was the real reason she'd left him with only that damned note? Whatever it was, he was going to find out. Perhaps when they were on Skye?

He turned to stare out the window. It was hot and there was a hint of thunder in the air. The weather matched his mood.

She had run from him once and he wasn't going to let her run again. At least until he was sure that she was running for the right reasons.

CHAPTER EIGHT

CASSIE WAS ANXIOUS as she packed for the weekend away in Skye with Leith. Whatever he thought about her having a way with children, those children were her patients. How could anyone not be kind to a child who was ill?

But this was different. Peter was Leith's son and he was expecting her to interact with him without the safety barrier of her profession. One of the reasons she'd walked away from Leith was that she didn't want to get too involved. Yet here she was, doing exactly what she'd promised herself she'd never do.

However, it was too late to back out now. She could hardly send Leith a text to say she'd changed her mind at this late stage. What had possessed her to agree?

She knew why. A little boy with the saddest eyes she had ever seen.

She folded a dress into her small carry-on bag

with an impatient sigh and followed it with a pair of sandals and then, as an afterthought, a pair of wellington boots.

One long weekend. Four days. After that Leith was on his own.

They took a flight to Glasgow, where Leith hired a car to drive the rest of the way. Peter sat in the back, either playing on his games console or watching DVDs on the portable player Leith had bought for him.

He still didn't talk much, but when he did he was polite. Hopefully, soon he would come to trust Leith the way he seemed to trust her.

When they got to Loch Lomond they stopped so they could show Peter the boats on the water.

Peter got out of the car, gave the loch a dutiful look as if to say, So what? and turned to Cassie. 'Can we go?'

Cassie saw the look of despair on Leith's face but to his credit he quickly masked it and just held open the back door for his son before strapping him into his car seat.

It was the same when they stopped in Glencoe. Despite the creepy grandeur of the mountains,

Peter only glanced up once before returning his attention back to his games console.

'Do you know there was a very famous battle here?' Cassie said, twisting around in her seat. 'Between two famous Scottish clans—the Campbells and the MacDonalds.'

He raised his head with the first sign of interest Cassie had seen. 'Did people get killed?'

She suppressed a smile as she slid a glance at Leith. This probably wasn't the kind of stuff one told timid six-year-olds but at least she had his attention.

'Quite a few,' she said. 'You see, what happened was…' And she went on to relay a very much censored story of the Campbells' perfidy towards the MacDonalds. 'You know, Peter, even these days some MacDonalds won't speak to a Campbell.'

Peter looked thoughtful. 'That's just silly,' he scoffed. 'People shouldn't be angry about something that happened before they were even born.'

'Which is why you shouldn't be angry about things that happened between Mummy and Daddy before you were born,' Leith said.

Cassie closed her eyes and suppressed a groan.

Just when she thought they were getting somewhere, along came Leith, putting his foot in it.

'And when we get to Skye,' Cassie said hastily, noticing that Peter's mouth had turned down at the corners and he was glaring at his father, 'I shall tell you stories about the fairy people who some people believe live there.'

Leith shot her a surprised look. 'I didn't realise you'd been to Skye.'

'I haven't. I read a couple of books as soon as I knew I was coming with you. I like to know my way around a country before I get there. I like to be prepared. No nasty surprises.'

Leith's eyes were dancing. 'Another country,' he repeated. 'Aye, well, I suppose many of the English do think of Scotland as being another country.'

'That's not what I meant,' Cassie retorted. Then she smiled. 'Admittedly, what I read about Skye does make it sound almost like another country. I'm looking forward to seeing it.' She turned back to Peter, who'd clearly been listening intently to the conversation. He dropped his gaze back to his game, but not quite soon enough—she'd seen the glint of interest in his eyes.

She widened her own in mock horror. 'There's a castle with a horrible dungeon and its very own fairy flag. I don't know about you, but I'd like to see that. But if we do, I'm going to need a brave boy to stop me from being scared. Do you know where I could find such a boy?'

Peter studied her for a moment. Then he nodded slowly and she caught a glimmer of a smile. 'I'll look after you. I'm not scared of *anything*.'

'Then you must be very brave because I'm scared of lots of things and so is your daddy.'

Peter stared at her in disbelief.

'He's terrified of spiders. Once one jumped on his shoulder and your dad nearly jumped out of his skin.'

'Hey,' Leith protested, 'you promised not to tell anyone about that.'

But Peter seemed pleased. 'Can we go to see the dungeon?' he asked.

'Sure. Perhaps tomorrow. You, me and your dad.'

Peter pursed his lips. 'Just you.'

Before Leith could say anything, Cassie jumped in. 'If that's what you want, that's fine by me. But let's see how we feel tomorrow, okay?'

* * *

When they arrived in Staffin, Peter was fast asleep.

The journey across Skye, from the point they'd crossed the bridge that joined the island to the mainland, had been breathtaking. There was something almost other-worldly about the deep glens surrounded by high mountains with their ridges like the spines of prehistoric animals. Cassie had the immediate impression of lives being lived here for generations and a sense of how life went on. The thought was comforting.

Leith slid her a look almost as if he could read her mind. 'Makes you feel small and immortal at the same time, doesn't it?' he said.

'Almost as if you could believe in magic and fairies.'

It was the first time in a long time that she'd seen Leith look so relaxed. Perhaps it was having his son with him, or perhaps it was coming home to the place he'd known all his life. Whatever it was, it was good for him.

What would it be like to feel that sense of belonging? To feel connected to a place? To know that, wherever you were in the world, there were people who longed to see you?

It had to feel wonderful.

Leith's parents were waiting for them at the door of their house and Cassie could see the family resemblance immediately. Although his father was developing a slight stoop, he was, or had been, as tall as Leith and had the same deep green eyes.

And when his mother came forward, holding out her hand and introducing herself as Maggie and her husband as Robbie, Cassie instantly recognised the smile she'd seen so often on Leith's face.

Leith shook hands with his father then picked his mother up, swinging her round and making her giggle.

'Oh, son,' she said, 'you've no idea how wonderful it is to have you home with us. Now, where's the little lad we've been hearing so much about?'

'He's asleep in the car,' Leith said. 'He's been asleep since we hit Kyle of Lochalsh. I suspect that's him out for the night.'

'I think it's better if we take him upstairs to his room without waking him,' Cassie suggested. 'He'll probably find all the new faces a little overwhelming. And if he's tired, he's bound to get cranky.'

'Good idea,' Maggie said straight away. 'I've made a bed up for him in the room next to yours, Leith. You're opposite, Cassie, if that's all right. I did wonder if you and Leith wanted to be together. If so, I can sort that out easily enough.'

Cassie sent Leith a startled look. When he raised an eyebrow and grinned she shook her head and frowned at him. He'd no right to even hint to his parents that they were a couple. Happily, his parents were peering through the car window, trying to get a glimpse of Peter, and didn't notice.

Leith's grin grew wider. 'No, Mother, Cassie will be fine where she is. We're just colleagues.' He wriggled his raised eyebrow. 'And friends?' It was more of a question than a statement and Cassie nodded. They were friends, she acknowledged. At least, as much friends as she ever allowed anyone to be.

Leith opened the car door and gently scooped

his son into his arms. 'Let me get Peter upstairs and settled and then we can catch up properly.'

Cassie followed Leith up the staircase to the first floor, noticing as they climbed that each window had spectacular views out to the sea and cliffs. The moon was high in the sky, casting a silvery glow.

'It doesn't quite get dark at this time of year,' Leith said. 'We have blackout curtains in most of the bedrooms so the light doesn't wake folk up too early.'

In that case, Cassie wouldn't be drawing hers. She hated waking from one of her nightmares in the dark.

'It will be better to leave the curtains open for Peter too,' she said. She paused. She remembered once, when she'd been sent away by her adoptive parents for some imagined misdemeanour, waking up in a strange bedroom with children she didn't know and adults who, although not unkind, had frightened her.

Actually, frightened was too weak a word. Terrified was closer to it. She'd been petrified of making a mistake or saying the wrong thing—anything that might prevent her from being sent home. Because whatever and however her parents behaved towards her, it had been home and she would have done anything to get back there. 'I think I should stay with him. At least for tonight. He might be frightened if he wakes up and doesn't know where he is.'

Leith looked at her strangely. 'He only has to call and I'll hear him. I'm right next door.'

But Cassie shook her head. 'I'd rather stay with him—honestly.'

'You care about him, don't you?'

Cassie pulled the duvet over Peter's shoulders and bent to kiss him on the temple. 'No child should ever be frightened,' she murmured.

'Cassie…' Leith's voice was low.

She kept her back to him. 'Goodnight, Leith. I'll see you in the morning.'

CHAPTER NINE

WHEN CASSIE AWOKE it was still very early—not quite six. Yet the sun was streaming in through the opened curtains, the rays settling on Peter's bed.

Quietly she checked to see whether he was still sleeping. He was staring up at the ceiling with his troubled green eyes, Mr Mouse clutched firmly in the crook of his arm.

'Morning, sweetheart,' Cassie whispered. 'Are you ready to get up now?'

Peter held out his arms and she scooped the warm and sweet-smelling body onto her lap. She hugged him tightly as he snuggled closer. 'This is your daddy's house. Do you remember us telling you?'

He nodded.

'And you remember we told you Daddy's own mummy and daddy—your grandparents—live here? They're really looking forward to seeing you. Is that okay?'

Peter nodded again.

'Now, why don't we get you dressed and then we'll go and explore. We can see the sea from the garden. Would you like to have a look?'

Another nod. More vigorous this time.

'Daddy?' Peter said. Cassie smiled. It was good he was finally willing to ask about his father. Now, if only she could stop Leith from expecting too much from his son, they might even get somewhere before the long weekend was over.

She helped Peter dress quickly and then took him through to her room while she did the same. He climbed up on the window seat and knelt, fists pressed into his neck, to stare out the window.

As soon as Cassie had pulled on her jeans and T-shirt she joined him. The gardens stretched into the distance—the sea glinting sapphire blue in the early morning sun.

'Are you ready?' she asked. When Peter nodded she took him by the hand. 'Shall we see if Daddy wants to come too?'

Peter looked at her for a long moment before shaking his head.

Cassie sighed inwardly. Perhaps by being here she was preventing Peter from bonding with his father? She reminded herself what it would be like to be a little child in an alien place surrounded by strangers. It was quite possible that he thought he was being punished. It's what she would have thought at the same age. No, if Leith wanted a relationship with his son and she had no reason to doubt that he did, it was up to him to find a way to his child. In the meantime, she couldn't—not in a million years—abandon the little boy.

They tiptoed downstairs and left by the unlocked front door. The moment they stepped outside the salt air hit Cassie and she closed her eyes. After the heat and traffic fumes of London, it felt fabulous. Above them an eagle stooped and swirled. Peter watched with his thumb in his mouth and then suddenly he smiled. He looked so like Leith it made her heart splinter.

'Come on, then, Peter, let's see what else we can discover before breakfast.'

* * *

From his bedroom window, Leith watched his son look up at Cassie and smile. Would his child ever feel half as easy with him as he did with Cassie? It was as if they'd recognised something in each other from the moment they'd met.

Just as he'd felt the first time he'd met her. How he still felt.

He was in love with her.

He had always been in love with her.

Hell.

Holding hands, Cassie and Peter were racing towards the sea. Instantly, Leith was out of the door. He should have warned Cassie last night. How could he have been so stupid?

As they got closer to the bit where the land seemed to disappear, Cassie stopped running.

'We have to be very careful,' she said to Peter. 'I think there's a very steep cliff here. You must never come here on your own. Okay?'

''Kay.' As a bird hopped over the grass, searching for worms, Peter let go of her hand and scampered after it.

'Stop!'

The shout came from behind them and Cassie whirled round to find Leith running towards them. Peter stopped chasing the bird, looked at his father and stuck his thumb back in his mouth. He started walking back to Cassie.

'Don't go any further,' Leith shouted. 'Not a step.'

Cassie's head swirled and all of a sudden she was standing miles away on a dusty road in Afghanistan, in the middle of a nightmare.

Leith moved as carefully as he could. Since he'd called out, Cassie had remained rooted to the spot, her eyes staring blankly somewhere beyond his right shoulder. Why didn't she walk towards him? Or reach for Peter?

A few steps away from her, his son had stopped in his tracks and was looking at Cassie, as if expecting her to tell him what to do. Why didn't she react?

If Peter continued towards her, his added weight could send the piece of overhanging cliff she was standing on plummeting down.

He forced away the image of the two people he

loved most in the world falling to their deaths. He couldn't show his panic. It would only make Peter run for the shelter of Cassie's arms. And if he ran towards his child, intercepting his son's path to Cassie, Peter might turn and run towards the cliff.

Leith hunkered down and held out his hand to his son. 'Peter, could you come to me?' he said, forcing his voice to sound calm.

Peter shook his head and took a step towards Cassie.

'Please, Peter. You need to walk to me. I have something I'd like you to see.'

For a moment he thought his ruse had worked and that Peter's natural curiosity would get the better of his reluctance to come to him, but in the next second, when Peter started running towards Cassie, he knew he'd failed.

He hurled himself towards them.

Suddenly Cassie felt herself being picked up and carried before she was unceremoniously dropped to the ground. She screamed in terror, vaguely aware of another cry that seemed to be coming from far away.

She was lying in a tangled heap of arms and legs.

Peter was crying, his squirming body trapped underneath hers. Leith was sprawled next to them, breathing deeply, his face white.

She wasn't in Afghanistan. She was in Skye. With Leith. She was safe.

'What the hell?' she said as soon as she got her breath back. She sat up·and held out her arms for Peter, who came willingly. 'Shh, Peter. It's okay.' She turned back to Leith. 'What on earth did you do that for? You terrified us both.'

She looked around. They were a good bit away from where they'd been standing. At least fifty yards. He must have carried them both all that way.

'You were standing on an overhang. We expect it to fall into the sea any time. I should have warned you. If I hadn't seen you...' Leith got to his feet. 'I called out. Why didn't you answer me?'

She scrambled to her feet with Peter still in her arms. 'I have no idea what you're talking about,' she said, trying not to flinch under his blistering gaze.

'You went as white as a sheet. I thought Peter was going to go to you and his weight, along with yours, would make the cliff crumble.'

She should have stopped Peter. Gone to him. And she hadn't.

Because she'd been transported back to Afghanistan and she'd frozen. Again.

Her teeth were chattering, her legs felt boneless. She needed to get away before she lost it. Leith looked down at her, clearly puzzled.

'I...I had no idea we were in danger,' Cassie said. To her mortification her voice was shaking.

'I'm going to have to get that part of the croft fenced off. I grew up with it so it didn't even occur to me to warn you about it.' He frowned. 'How am I supposed to remember all of it? Isn't there a damn book I can buy? Some sort of manual that tells you what to do and what not to do—something that reminds you what to watch out for?'

He looked so bewildered that Cassie's heart went out to him. 'You're doing just fine,' she said softly. 'You weren't to know I would take Peter for a walk.'

'No, but I should have warned you anyway. Next time check with one of us before you take off. Skye is full of steep cliffs that fall away suddenly and without warning.'

Cassie really, really needed to be on her own. She placed Peter on the ground, took his hand and Leith's and joined them.

'Perhaps it's time you started learning. I'm going for a walk. You should take Peter back inside.'

Before Leith could protest, she'd turned on her heel and was striding away across the moors.

Leith took Peter back to the house, the little boy trotting uncomplainingly by his side. Strange that his son should choose this time to trust his father.

'Is Cassie angry with me?' Peter asked quietly.

Leith stopped and crouched next to his son. 'Cassie would never be angry with you. She just got a fright.'

'You rescued me from the sea… And Cassie.'

'You…' He was about to lie to Peter—tell him

that he'd been in no danger—but he decided against it. That wasn't the way it was going to be between him and his child. 'I wasn't going to let anything happen to you. I love you. I promise to keep you safe. It's my job. Do you understand?'

Peter nodded. 'You, me and Cassie. We keep each other safe.'

Leith's chest felt tight. He resisted the urge to crush his child to him. 'Yes, son. Now I'll take you to meet your grandmother. When I'm sure you're okay, I'm going to see if Cassie is all right.'

'I told you. I'm a big boy. You can leave me alone. Mummy used to leave me alone sometimes and nothing ever happened. I don't get scared. Not even when it's dark.'

Leith's anger towards Jude rose. How could she leave a child of six on his own? He forced a smile. 'You know what, Peter? Even though you are a big, brave boy, I'm never going to leave you on your own. Not until you're as tall as me anyway.'

Peter took his hand. 'I grow fast. I'm almost up to your waist already.'

'So you are. But don't grow too fast, son.'

Back at the house his mother was up and in the kitchen.

'You two must have been up early.' She smiled at them. 'Hello, Peter. I'm your daddy's mum. I know you have another granny so you can call me Granny Skye if you like.'

Peter studied her for a few moments. 'You've got white hair.'

'So I have,' she agreed. 'Are you ready for some breakfast?'

Peter nodded.

'Then why don't you take a seat at the table and after breakfast we can go and fetch some more eggs for baking?'

To Leith's relief, Peter did as she asked. He wanted to go in search of Cassie. Something was very wrong—she would never have left Peter after what had happened if it wasn't. But he didn't want to leave his son. Especially not now.

'Where's Cassie?' His mother asked. 'Still in bed?'

'No, she's up too. She's out on the croft.'

'She got a fright,' Peter said. He looked at Leith. 'You better find her in case she gets lost.'

'Will you be all right here with Granny Skye?'

Peter hesitated. He looked at his grandmother then back to Leith. He popped his thumb in his mouth then took it out again. 'I'll be good. You need to go and get Cassie.'

Cassie stared out at the waves crashing onto the rocks. Although she'd walked the terror out of her head, she wasn't ready to return to the house.

She should have gone back with Leith and Peter. The little boy had just had a scare. He'd needed her. Yet she hadn't been able to do it. Her need to be on her own had been too overwhelming.

If ever she needed evidence that she wasn't up to the job of parenting, even on a minor scale, she'd just had it.

When she heard a footfall behind her, she knew it was Leith. It was as if her body had its own radar as far as he was concerned. Reluctantly she turned to face him.

'You okay?' he asked.

'Why do you keep asking me that?' she replied.

'Because clearly you're not. Something isn't

right. You seem different from the Cassie I knew on the ship.'

'We all change, Leith. It wouldn't say much about us if we didn't.' But she hadn't changed. She was still the not-quite-up-to-it Cassie she'd always been. Surely Leith could see that now?

'It's not just that,' he said. 'Sometimes you look so sad. Lost even.'

Sad? Lost? She couldn't bear it if that's how he saw her.

'I can't make you out, Cassie.' He touched her on the shoulder, his warm hands sliding up towards her neck. 'You're still trembling.'

It took every ounce of her willpower not to bolt from the intimacy of his touch. Confusingly, at the same time she wanted to throw herself into his arms and rest against him for a while.

She sucked in a breath. 'Being here,' she began, 'brings back memories, and not pleasant ones.'

'I'm not sure I understand. You've never been here before.'

'Oh, it's not the place,' Cassie admitted. 'It's your family—the way you obviously all love each other and are desperate for Peter to know that he is loved too. I suspect you would walk to the ends of the earth if you thought it would make him happy.'

Her team in Afghanistan had been like her family.

'Your parents don't love you?'

Cassie laughed—but even to her own ears it wasn't a happy sound. 'Not every family is like yours, you know.'

'Come on, Cassie. That's not good enough. Talk to me. Tell me about them. We're friends, aren't we?'

Friends? Friends! Was the man completely oblivious to the way she felt about him?

He folded his arms. 'I'm not going anywhere until you talk to me.'

She wrapped her arms around herself. 'There's nothing really to tell. I was adopted. I never really got on with my adoptive parents. They spend half the year in South Africa so I don't see much of them.' Didn't see them at all, if she was honest. She shrugged. 'That's all there is to it. At least you want to be a good father to Peter. You want him to be happy.'

'Of course I do,' Leith said. 'But wanting to make him happy isn't the same thing as knowing how to. Cassie, this dad stuff is harder, much harder, than my own dad made—makes it look. Perhaps you should cut your adoptive parents some slack?'

Cassie had to smile. 'You'll learn,' she said dryly. 'And no one can say you're not trying.'

Leith's eyes searched her face and she turned away. Like always, it was as if he were looking right into her soul. She didn't want him to see what was really there. That would have been too much.

'Look, could we leave it?' she said before he could probe further.

She felt his hands on her shoulders and he turned her so she was facing him. The world stopped turning as he placed his hands on either side of her face.

'Talk to me, Cassie.'

She shook her head, unable to speak.

He lowered his head and his lips were on hers. She clung to him, unable to stop herself giving in to the oblivion of his kiss.

When she pulled away, his eyes were glinting. 'I knew I wasn't wrong back on the Mercy Ship and I'm not wrong now. There was something between us then and it's still there. I know you feel it too. For God's sake, Cassie, don't keep pushing me away.'

It was as if someone had pierced her heart with a shard of glass. He had no idea how much she wanted to go back to the way it had been. How it had been when she'd thought there might be a future for them. The time before Peter.

She stepped away. 'We're colleagues. That's all. I shouldn't have kissed you. You caught me off guard, that's all.' She forced a smile. 'Now I think I'll go to my room.'

His dark, questioning eyes were still on her. The last time he'd looked at her like that had been eighteen months ago—just before they'd made love for the first time. Her chest tightened and she spun on her heel and hurried back to the house as fast as she could. But not before she thought she heard him call her name.

Leith watched as Cassie disappeared behind the trees that shielded the house from the main road.

He frowned. She'd been fast but not fast enough to hide the desire in her eyes when he'd touched her. It was the same look he'd seen all those months ago, the same longing he was sure had been reflected in his own eyes. He'd bet his life that she cared for him. But, then, he would have said the same thing eighteen months ago, and he'd been wrong.

He'd seen the desire, but he'd also seen the pain and heard it in her voice. What had happened to her in the time since they'd seen each other? If she'd been reserved when they'd first met, she was even more shut off now. Something—or someone—had hurt Cassie, and badly.

And one way or another he was going to find out what—or who—it had been.

After the excitement of earlier, breakfast was a reassuringly casual and relaxed affair. To Cassie's surprise and relief, Peter seemed unaffected by what had happened earlier. When she'd returned, he'd run to her and wrapped his arms around her knees but then he'd gone back to helping Maggie lay the table.

After they finished eating, Maggie invited her grandson to go and look for some fresh eggs with her, and after only the smallest hesitation the little boy took her hand and allowed himself to be led from the room.

It was going better than she'd hoped. Peter seemed more comfortable around women, which was probably only to be expected, but he was clearly beginning to relax with Leith's family. It was just a pity that Leith couldn't always bring him to Skye—at least, until the child had familiarised himself with his father. Then she wouldn't be needed.

The thought didn't give her as much pleasure as she'd imagined it would.

Peter was smiling proudly when he returned with three brown eggs in his basket. Solemnly he lifted one from his basket and handed it to Cassie. Then he gave another one to his grandmother. Finally he turned to his father and everyone in the room held their breath. Cassie prayed that Leith wouldn't do anything that would startle the boy.

When Peter reached into his basket for the only remaining egg and held it out to Leith, Cassie let her breath out—she hadn't even realised she'd been holding it.

'Is that for me?' Leith asked quietly.

Peter seemed uncertain for a moment, as if thinking of changing his mind. Then he nodded and Leith accepted the egg with the same gravity he gave to his patients when they were telling him their symptoms.

'Shall I keep it? Or have it for my breakfast?' he asked.

'Keep it,' Peter said, 'until it hatches.'

Cassie hid a smile at the look of consternation on Leith's face. But then, even before he opened his mouth to reply, she just knew he was about to say the wrong thing.

'I don't think it will hatch, son. You see, an egg needs to be kept warm by its mother before it can become a chicken.' Oops. That was so not the right thing to say. As Peter thrust out his lower lip, Cassie shot Leith a warning glance and said quickly, 'We'll get you a box to keep it in—for a few days.'

It seemed from the dawning realisation on Leith's face that he was beginning to catch on. 'But when we go, perhaps we'd better leave it with the mother hen? They might miss one another.' Leith shot Cassie a triumphant smile.

Peter's face crumpled and he threw Cassie an

anguished look before bolting from the room. As Leith's mother went to follow, Cassie got to her feet too. She shook her head at Leith.

'Not your smartest move,' she said wryly, 're-minding him that he's not with his mother.' And leaving a bewildered Leith staring at his father, Cassie hurried after Peter and his grandmother.

It was the nightmare again. It was never quite the same. She'd be walking along, laughing at something her companion had said. Sometimes it would be Angela, sometimes Linda—it changed from night to night.

Then suddenly there would be a blinding flash, a shock of heat and she'd be thrown up in the air.

When she came to all she heard was an eerie stillness where only minutes before there had been the sound of children's laughter and moth-ers' scolding.

She'd tried to move, but couldn't. She tried to talk but her mouth was caked with dust.

She looked over to where Angela should be and when she saw the crumpled, still form, she tried again to make her limbs move. She rolled over on her stomach—a feat requiring a gargantuan effort. She had to take a few moments to rest before, using her elbows, she crawled inch by painful inch towards her injured colleague.

And then...

'Cassie, what is it?'

She struggled to open her eyes. Where was she? There was something she had to do but she couldn't think what it was.

She tried to get out of bed but strong arms held her back.

'I have to help...' Cassie shouted, trying to push the arms away. Her heart pounded harder. She thought she could hear the sound of it beating.

'Cassie, you're dreaming. You're in Skye. Come on, wake up.' The arms held her loosely, as if knowing that pulling her closer would only make her feel more frightened. 'It's Leith, Cassie.'

Her heart was beginning to slow down. 'Leith?' What was he doing here?

'You're okay. You've just had a bad dream. You're safe now.'

Although her heart was still pounding painfully, the nightmare was beginning to recede.

She wasn't in Afghanistan. There was no one calling for her. She wasn't too frightened to move.

But Linda was still dead.

She gave a little moan and this time Leith's arms did tighten around her. She let herself lean into him. Just for a moment. All of a sudden the feeling of his arms around her—the same, safe feeling she'd always had when with him—triggered something in her and she found herself sobbing against his chest, deep, racking sobs that seemed to come from a place so deep inside that she hadn't known it existed. Hot tears coursed down her face, filling her mouth with salty wetness. She hadn't known it was even possible to cry like this. But she couldn't stop herself.

He didn't say anything. Apart from a hand that came up to stroke her hair, he hardly seemed to move a muscle.

Eventually she managed to get herself under control. She pulled away from him, grabbed a bunch of tissues from the bedside table and hid her face in them.

What on earth had come over her? She'd never lost it like this before and certainly not in front of anyone. And that it should be Leith made it worse.

'Do you want to tell me what that was about?' he asked gently once she'd blown her nose.

She was glad that the room was dark so he couldn't see her face. 'I was shouting in my sleep, huh?' she said. 'Sorry if I woke you.'

'I'm a light sleeper.'

He would have had to be a very light sleeper to have heard her through the thick walls—or she'd been crying out louder than usual.

'It's time you talked to me.'

Cassie shook her head. She drew her knees up to her chest and suppressed a shiver.

'I'm not leaving until you do,' Leith said quietly. She felt the bed shift under his weight as he stretched himself out next to her. The length of his body was immediately familiar—almost as if the intervening time hadn't passed. 'Talking about it might help chase the demons away.'

Cassie doubted that any amount of talking could chase away her particular demons, but maybe it was the darkness of the room with only a sliver of light from the moon, perhaps it was the warmth of Leith's body next to hers and the fact that he didn't try to touch her, but without even knowing she was going to do it, she started talking.

'It was a normal day. Hot. But it was always hot in Afghanistan. We were based at a camp where the army has a medical facility. We weren't treating soldiers—just using it as a base.'

'Go on,' he said.

'There were five of us. Me, a paediatric surgeon, two nurses and an interpreter. Our remit was to carry out clinics and surgery if necessary at the local hospital. Although it sounds dangerous, we didn't think it would be. We were civilians and doctors and nurses. The hospital was well protected too. Just in case. I wasn't at all frightened. I was excited.'

'Cassie, I had no idea you were planning to go there. The last time we spoke you said the UN was sending you to Sudan.'

'They did and I went. But when the opportunity came to go out to Afghanistan I jumped at the chance.'

She paused. 'I guess part of me wanted to prove that I was at least as brave as my adoptive mother.' She managed a smile. 'In my thirties and still trying to impress parents who I didn't even see.'

She felt Leith take her hand. He gave it a gentle squeeze.

'But it wasn't just that. I'd read how much the civilians needed medical help.' She sucked in a breath. She wasn't quite ready to tell him that the time she'd spent working on the Mercy Ship had been the happiest of her life—mainly because of him, but also because she'd found that what she'd been doing had made her feel truly good about herself.

For the first time she hadn't been trying to be what she thought her adopted parents wanted her to be—she hadn't been trying to be the best, the best in her class, the best in her year, the student and trainee who impressed everyone she came across. She had just tried to do the best job she could with what she'd had. Could Leith even begin to understand what it was like to be her? She was sure he'd never doubted himself in his life—or felt the need to prove himself.

'Anyway, we went out. We received some training from the army—what to do if we were attacked, or kidnapped, that sort of thing. But they made it clear that we would only be allowed to go to the hospital if they were certain it was safe.'

'Go on.' His voice was quiet but she was intensely aware of him. Although, apart from his hand, his body wasn't touching hers, she felt heat and energy radiating from him.

'The first few weeks were fine. The five of us made a good team.' Her voice cracked. The truth was she'd become closer to them than she'd ever been to her own family—apart from Martha, of course. 'Then one day, when we only had a couple of weeks left...' her breath hitched '...everything went wrong.'

As she thought back to that day her heartbeat quickened. 'As usual, we'd been taken to right outside the hospital by an armoured vehicle. They always dropped us off then patrolled outside until we were ready to leave. One of our regular escorts was a young captain called Linda. It was her last tour. She was going back to get married. She was so much in love.'

Cassie closed her eyes. It was unbelievable to recall now the envy she'd felt for Linda—to have found her soul mate and to be so certain that their future together would be for ever…

'Anyway, one of the nurses, Angela, hated the fact that there were always scrawny, half-starved dogs outside the hospital. She must have seen one she wanted to give a titbit to as she wandered off—at least, I think that's what happened. I heard Linda call out to her, telling her to come back, and the next thing I knew there was this almighty explosion. It was as if the world had stopped turning. For what seemed like hours but could have only been seconds there was this deathly silence. I didn't even feel any pain until much later. Some small pieces of shrapnel had lodged in my side. All I could see was a bundle of what looked like rags. There was a whimpering noise and I knew that Angela had been badly injured.'

Her throat tightened, making it difficult to speak. But Leith said nothing, simply increasing the pressure on her hand.

'To cut a long story short, I wanted to go to her, but Linda shouted at me to stay where I was. And then…' She didn't know if she could finish. In her mind she saw again the crumpled body on the ground, the shocked and empty silence, a bird hovering overhead. 'And then Linda took a step towards Angela and there was another explosion. And that's all I remember until I woke up back in the hospital at camp.'

'The nurse, did she make it?' Leith asked softly.

'Yes she did, thank goodness. It turned out that the dog she'd been following had set off the first IED. But there was another one and Linda…' She drew a deep, shuddering breath. 'She didn't stand a chance.'

This time she allowed Leith to take her into his arms and as the tears came she let herself relax against his chest. 'Why did it have to be her? She had everything to look forward to.'

Leith's hands were in her hair and he was murmuring words of comfort. Cassie pulled away from him. 'Don't you see?' she burst out. 'It should have been me.'

'But that's ridiculous,' Leith said. 'It wasn't your fault.'

'I can't help feeling guilty. If I had moved first Linda wouldn't have stood on the mine.'

'That's crazy thinking, Cassie! There could

have been other mines. Linda was a trained soldier. She would have been trained to act instinctively and would have known the risks. On the other hand, you were a civilian. You did the right thing by listening to her instructions.'

'Linda was only there because she was protecting us,' Cassie replied bitterly. 'Why did she die and we survive?'

There was a silence for a while. 'I never thought I'd hear Cassie Ross feeling sorry for herself. I never put self-pity and you together somehow.'

Cassie felt as if she'd been slapped. What did he mean? She was only telling him how she saw it.

'I'm not looking for your sympathy,' she said stiffly.

'Just as well because you're not going to get it. At least, not for the reasons you think. You deserve sympathy for what happened out there. It was a horrific experience for anyone to go through and I can't even begin to imagine what it must have been like for you. But to hold yourself responsible... No, Cassie, that smacks of self-pity and I suspect Linda deserves more than that from you.'

'But if it weren't for us…if I hadn't ignored her warning and moved towards the nurse, Linda wouldn't have felt she had to intervene. She wouldn't have died.'

'It sounds to me that Linda was a very brave woman who was doing the job she'd signed up for. I don't think you are doing her memory any favours by rewriting the whole episode from your point of view.'

'Is that what you think I'm doing?' Fury bubbled up inside her. 'Do you know what it's like to relive something in your head every day, knowing that if only you could have sixty seconds over again it could all be different? Do you know what it's like to dream about it, night after night? To wake yourself up screaming with terror?'

'No, I don't. But it will pass, Cassie. Trust me, it will pass.'

He tucked the blanket under her chin, much the same way she'd seen him do with Peter. Then he pulled her against him and she could hear the beating of his heart.

'Go back to sleep,' he said softly.

'You don't have to stay.'

'Don't argue, woman. I'm not going anywhere.'

And as she drifted off to sleep she thought she heard him murmur, 'Not ever again.'

Leith held Cassie as her breathing deepened and she fell into what he hoped was a dreamless sleep.

At least she was beginning to talk to him. What had happened to her in Afghanistan explained a lot—her haunted look, the way she'd frozen that morning on the cliff. But that didn't explain everything. There was more she was hiding from him. Stuff he needed to discover about her if there was the remotest chance for them to have a future together.

God, he loved this woman—this complicated, prickly, defensive, proud woman. The thought that she'd been hurt, inside and out, and he hadn't been there for her churned him up inside and he vowed that she would never have to face anything alone again. Not while there was breath in his body.

Without really knowing it, he had been waiting for her to come back to him. And if he had to wait another eighteen months, or even eighteen years, so be it.

* * *

Cassie slept deeply and dreamlessly for the rest of that night and awoke feeling refreshed and at peace. It seemed Leith had been right. Talking about what had happened had helped.

Or was it just that being around Leith made her feel safe? As if nothing bad could ever happen to her again?

He was still stretched out beside her. Quietly, so as not to wake him, she propped herself on her elbow and studied him. Even in sleep there was a small smile tugging at the corners of his mouth.

He opened one eye. 'Morning.'

She blushed, embarrassed that he'd caught her staring. 'You didn't have to stay the whole night.'

'I wanted to be here in case you woke up again,' he said.

She threw the blankets aside and jumped out of bed. He stared at her for a few moments through narrowed eyes. 'Cute,' he said. 'Very cute. Aren't those panties you're wearing the same ones you almost lost the day you arrived at the ship?'

'Of course they aren't,' she retorted, knowing her face had to be scarlet. She almost leaped to the end of the bed where she'd left her dressing gown. Indeed, a world-class sprinter couldn't have left the starting blocks as fast as she'd just moved.

Leith eased his long legs over the side of the bed and came to stand beside her. Still grinning, he tied the belt of her dressing gown for her. 'Feel better now?'

Damn the man for knowing exactly the way he was making her feel. He could at least have the decency to pretend.

'I'm perfectly fine,' she said through stiff lips. As his smile broadened she had to laugh. She pulled her hair into a ponytail and smiled up at him. 'You know, Leith, I actually think I might be.'

When he left, she dressed, suffused with an energy she hadn't felt for a long time, grabbed some fruit from a bowl and let herself out of the house.

She walked until her legs ached. Up steep hills from where she could see the ocean stretching into the distance and then down into hidden valleys where she discovered small whitewashed cottages huddled against the hills. Thoughts of Leith filled her head. She could imagine them here together, living in one of the small croft houses, going for long walks along the shore before returning to their bed to make love.

Of course, her fantasies were just that. She was still in love with Leith, of course she was, she had never stopped loving him, but there was still the matter of Peter. She still couldn't see herself as a mother—not even a stepmother. As for Leith… The time hadn't been right for them when they'd first met, and it wasn't right now—even if she knew she could never love anyone the way she loved him.

Nevertheless, by the time she'd returned to the house, she felt happier than she could remember. Certainly since the weeks on board ship.

She sniffed the air. Something smelled delicious. Following the aromas to the kitchen, she found Leith in the armchair by the Aga, reading a book to Peter, who was perched somewhat precariously on the arm. Leith's father was doing a crossword while his mother was kneading something in a large bowl.

'I wish I could bake,' Cassie said.

'You can't bake?' Maggie asked incredulously.

'Never learned. I suspect it's too late now.'

'Wheesh. Away with you! It's never too late,' Maggie replied. 'I was just about to start a batch of scones. Why don't you help me and I'll show you it's not as difficult as you think?' She glanced around and finding an apron handed it to Cassie.

Peter, she noticed, had slid down the arm of the chair and was now half on and half off Leith's lap. Leith shifted slightly to let his son make himself more comfortable.

Leith's mother showed her how to rub butter into flour before mixing it with milk to form a dough.

'Now we roll it out lightly and cut it into rounds.' Maggie looked over at Peter. 'Would you like to help?'

But to Cassie's delight Peter shook his head and snuggled deeper into Leith.

When Leith glanced up, her heart shifted as she read the pleasure in his eyes. He and his son were going to be all right.

After the scones were in the oven, Maggie

started teaching Cassie how to make a clootie dumpling.

'It's called clootie because it's cooked in a cloth—a clootie. It takes a few hours of steaming but it's worth it.'

Leith had finished the story by this time and Peter had slipped off his lap. Peter came across to the table, sat down and propped his chin on his hands.

Cassie carried on stirring fruit into the flour mixture. The first batch of scones was ready and Maggie took them out of the oven.

'What about you, Peter? Do you want a go at mixing?' Cassie asked.

Peter nodded and Cassie handed him a wooden spoon. He stood in the space between her arms and the table and began to mix. When Cassie looked up it was to find Leith's eyes on her and the look of love she saw there took her breath away.

But it was Peter who he was looking at, wasn't it? Not her.

That afternoon they took Peter to the castle to see the dungeon and Cassie made sure she appeared sufficiently frightened to make the little boy feel he was protecting her. When they'd finished at the castle, they went for a walk to the coral beach. The next day they walked to the Fairy Glen. As it was a beautiful, clear day, Maggie had packed a picnic for them.

After their walk Cassie unpacked the picnic basket while Leith threaded some worms onto a fishing rod.

'I don't believe in fairies,' Peter said suddenly. 'I'm too big a boy.'

'You're certainly a brave boy,' Cassie agreed.

Peter crept closer to her until he was leaning his head against her arm. 'I used to believe in Santa when I was little,' he confided.

Cassie hid a smile. 'You don't any more?'

'Last year he didn't come to my house.'

'He didn't?'

Cassie looked across at Leith, who had stopped what he was doing and was watching Peter intently.

'Why do you think that was?' she asked the little boy.

''Cos I wasn't a good enough boy to get presents. But the next day Mummy bought me a whole pile. So I knew then it wasn't Santa who brought the presents.'

Cassie's heart ached for him. This trying-to-be-good-but-never-believing-he-could-be-good-enough behaviour she recognised only too well.

Leith growled something under his breath and scowled.

'You know something, Peter,' Cassie said carefully. 'I don't think there's a better boy in the whole wide world than you.'

Peter huddled closer to Cassie. 'Do you believe in Santa?' he asked.

A lump formed in Cassie's throat. 'I believe magic can happen sometimes.' She picked a dandelion 'clock' from the long grass. 'Do you know, if you close your eyes and blow, you can make a wish? Some people believe the seeds are little fairies who then scatter to make your wish come true.'

Peter looked up at her. 'I told you I'm too big to believe in fairies.'

Cassie smiled at him. 'Then there's nothing to lose, is there? Why don't we give it a go?'

Peter hesitated before taking the dandelion from Cassie. He closed his eyes, pursed his lips and blew hard. The seeds, each with its own 'parachute', danced in the sunshine before dispersing in all directions.

'You know what I wished,' he said, opening his eyes and looking down at the ground. 'I wished you could always be with me.'

The lump in Cassie's throat made it difficult to speak. She forced herself not to look at Leith.

'Oh, Peter,' she said hoarsely, 'if you ever need me, close your eyes and think of me. That way, if I can't be with you in person, I'll be in your mind.'

That night, Cassie lay in bed, tossing and turning.

Peter's wish troubled her. At least the little boy was coming to trust his father; no longer demanding Cassie or his grandmother's presence at all times. That was the way it should be. It wasn't as if Cassie was going to be anything but a temporary figure in his life—whatever she'd promised.

Her heart stumbled. She was going to do to Peter what had been done to her so many times;

dance in and out of his life when what he really needed was constancy. Already the little boy was forming an attachment to her. It was one thing to care for the child over a few days, quite another being a stable, loving presence in his life day after day, year after year.

She wouldn't be around for very much longer. All too soon she'd be leaving. How could she bear to leave Leith again when the merest glimpse of him still sent shooting stars of desire along her nerve endings? When her nightmares had been replaced by fairy-tale dreams of the two of them in a cottage in a place pretty much like this—miles away from everywhere and everyone.

She pushed the images away. They'd be returning to London tomorrow. Leith was due to take Peter back to his maternal grandmother the following morning and soon her time at the practice would be coming to end. She closed her eyes as a shard of pain pierced her heart.

She thought back to the last few days. Leith and his family in the kitchen—the warmth, the love and the sheer enjoyment they had in each other's company. Being around Peter, Leith and his family made her feel good.

But it wasn't about her. It was about them.

CHAPTER TEN

A COUPLE OF weeks after their return from Skye, Cassie was in her consulting room, studying the blood-test results of one of her patients when there was a tap on the door and Leith walked in.

Cassie resented the way her heart flipped whenever she saw him. She repeatedly told herself that she would learn to live without him, and when the thought came into her head that she hadn't got over him in eighteen months, she ignored it. Being in love with someone was not the same as doing anything about it.

'Just to let you know everything is sorted for Friday. The duchess's secretary has emailed us both an itinerary. We fly out on a scheduled flight.'

'Sounds fine,' Cassie said. 'How's Peter?'

Leith smiled. 'He's great. His grandmother and aunt have noticed a difference in him. They say he's behaving more like the little boy he is rather than a miniature adult.' He perched on the edge of her desk. 'What's more, Jude's volunteered to go into rehab. Her mother and sister think she means to get off the drugs for good. Jude's told them it's time she sorted her life out so she can be a proper mother to Peter'

'But that's great, Leith! Peter deserves a mother in his life. A mother who loves him.'

Leith's expression turned serious. 'Have I said thank you?'

'What for?'

'For helping me with him. For making him feel safe to be with me. You'd make a great mother, Cassie.'

Would she? She'd never know. She averted her eyes. 'So what about these plans for the trip, then?'

On Friday morning Cassie was showered and dressed by six a.m. Leith hadn't mentioned her nightmare, but sometimes she would catch him looking at her, the expression in his eyes unreadable. Since that night she hadn't had the dream again. Instead, she fell asleep almost instantly, waking late and feeling refreshed and at peace.

However, last night she'd hardly slept. In the end she'd given up, pulled on her sweats and running shoes and let herself out into the drizzly London streets.

Why was she getting herself worked up about this trip anyway? They'd fly in, be around if they were needed and fly back on Tuesday. She didn't see what she and Leith were actually going to do for the four days they'd be there. The duchess's pregnancy was going well and given that she was only thirty-two weeks it was unlikely she'd be going into labour any time soon. It was also unlikely that the duchess would wish or expect Leith and Cassie to be with her every moment.

But it wasn't as if she would have to be with Leith all the time either. At least, she hoped not. These last few weeks had made one thing abundantly clear. She was in love with Leith and would be until the end of her days.

When she returned from her run, she showered and changed into her favourite sundress. As she applied her lipstick she studied herself in the mirror. She'd gained weight and the shadows under her eyes had all but disappeared. Being in love had something going for it.

Her packing finished, she snapped her bag shut and paused for a moment. She had everything. Her bikini, a good book to read and her guide book to the Caribbean. There were several things she wanted to see while she was there if she got the time. She really had no idea how these trips worked. Were they treated as guests or as the hired help? Frankly, she hoped it was the latter. The thought of having to make small talk with the duchess and her party horrified her.

Nevertheless, the knowledge that she would be the guest of a duchess gave her some kind of perverse pleasure. Her adoptive mother would have been thrilled to know that Cassie had anything to do with such exalted company.

A car hooted below and she picked up her case, locked the door behind her and ran downstairs. Leith was waiting for her in a black sports car. He leaped out and opened the boot, which was minuscule. When he saw her bag he grinned. 'I see you've learnt your lesson about packing—no chance of this suitcase spewing its contents all over the street.'

She laughed. 'It wasn't my most sophisticated moment, was it?'

'No one could say you didn't make a grand entrance.' He lowered his voice. 'Not that you needed to throw your underwear around to get my attention. You had it from the first moment I saw you.'

The world seemed to stop spinning. Cassie sucked in a breath. She wished he hadn't said that. She wished he wouldn't look at her as if she mattered. She wished— God, she wished she could be in his arms again. Safe and loved. She gave herself a mental shake, hoping that she didn't look as hot and bothered as she felt.

'Hadn't we better get going?' She was glad that her voice sounded normal—cool and amused even. She was damned if she was going to give him the slightest indication that he affected her the way he did. These next few days were going to be tough if every time she saw him or he spoke to her she was going to react like a school girl.

'All set?' he asked as he accelerated the car. She was unbearably conscious of his proximity, his thigh inches away from hers, the faint smell of his aftershave.

'This is a Lamborghini, isn't it?' Cassie asked.

'Four hundred horsepower, I'm guessing.' She had mastered the art of small talk. Keep conversation away from the personal and everything would be all right.

'You know your cars?' Leith asked.

'Always been a hobby of mine,' Cassie replied with a smile. 'I used to rally drive at one time.'

Leith whistled. 'Any other hidden talents you've kept from me?'

Cassie darted him a look. On the Mercy Ship she'd always turned the questions away from her—usually by diverting him with a touch of her fingertips or her lips or… Now she was getting hot and bothered again.

Wasn't the plan to keep the discussion away from her? She shook her head.

'No. I lead a dull life really.'

His mouth lifted at the corners. 'I'd hardly say that. The Mercy Ship then Sudan, followed by a near-death experience in Afghanistan. Most people don't experience what you have in a lifetime, let alone a couple of years.'

She flushed under the admiration in his dark eyes. Then it struck her. Leith knew more about her than any other person on the planet—and somehow that didn't scare her at all.

The island was beautiful with its whitewashed houses crammed up against the hill. The smell of olives and spices drifted on the heavy night air.

The duchess—'you must call me Veronica'—was relaxed and had an impish sense of humour.

'I do hope you won't be bored,' she said. 'I wouldn't have dragged you all the way out here if it hadn't been for my mother. She's so protective. But aren't mothers always?' Veronica looked at Cassie and she managed a smile in return.

'Now, I don't want you to feel tied to me. As long as I can get in touch with you by phone at any time, that's good enough for me. It's not as if this island is so huge you could ever be more than a few miles away anyway. On the other hand, you are most welcome to spend time with my party. It's just a few close friends. Mummy is here for a couple of days but she has to go back the day after tomorrow.'

'I wouldn't like to intrude,' Cassie murmured. 'To tell you the truth, I'm looking forward to catching up on some reading and doing some exploring.'

'I thought you might feel that way,' Veronica said, 'so I have arranged for you to stay in the Captain's Lookout—it's just a little distance from the main house but it has the most amazing views. It has everything you need—and someone to cook and clean—but if you'd rather stay at the main house, just say the word. And please come for dinner or lunch any time you wish. We are quite informal here.'

Staying somewhere with Leith wouldn't have been Cassie's choice but before she could say anything, Leith replied for them both.

'That sounds good to me. What about you, Cassie?' She could have sworn there was laughter in his eyes. Did he have any idea how much he unsettled her?

She feigned indifference. 'Whatever is easiest.' Despite Veronica's words, there was no way she could invite herself to stay at the main house. 'And please don't worry about entertaining us. I'm sure we will manage to look after ourselves.'

'Very well, but at least come for dinner on our

last night. Everyone will be there and we hope to make quite a party of it.'

'I'll be down to the house twice a day,' Leith said, 'to check up on you. Although I have to say I have no worries or concerns at all about the baby at the moment.'

Veronica flashed a smile. 'I feel like such a fraud. But having you here is reassuring for me as well as Mummy.'

If Veronica felt a fraud, where did that leave Cassie? The chances of her paediatric skills being needed were a thousand to one. Still, she was here and she might as well make the most of it.

Cassie was enchanted with the Captain's Lookout. It was built, a bit like the top of a lighthouse, with floor-to-ceiling windows. As Veronica had said, it was perched on top of a hill with a three-hundred-and-sixty degree view of the island—beaches on one side, forest on the other. The main house was fifty metres below, only a short walk away should they be needed, and was screened from view by a small wood.

Just behind their temporary home was a small building.

'That's where my wife and daughter, Tess, stay,' their driver said. 'My wife, Josie, is the cook and housekeeper. And whenever you want to go somewhere it will be my pleasure to take you. There isn't much to see, apart from the beaches, but there is one bar and a good restaurant down by the pier.'

'It sounds heavenly,' Cassie said.

'How long you here?'

'Just a few nights.'

'That is a shame. You should stay for at least two weeks. You tourists need time to relax, become like us islanders. You are always rushing, rushing.'

Cassie and Leith shared a smile. Cassie supposed the chauffeur was right. They were always rushing, rushing. At least, she was. Whenever she didn't have anything planned, a horrible restless energy would build up inside her. It was one of the reasons she sometimes ran until she was so exhausted she could hardly put one foot in front of the other.

Inside, the Captain's Lookout was even more breathtaking. Someone had kept the inside plain, with scrubbed wooden floors and simple leather furniture, the only colour coming from bright rugs strewn on the floor.

But it was the view from the bedroom that made Cassie gasp. Jutting out slightly on a small promontory and facing the sea, almost two-thirds of her bedroom walls were windows that framed the view. Apart from the boats bobbing in the bay, the sea, lit by a full moon, was a mass of aquamarine blue tipped with white. It wasn't difficult to imagine a sea captain looking out from here, watching for pirates. Cassie smiled. Now, where had that thought come from? Before she'd met Leith she hadn't been prone to romantic thoughts yet here she was daydreaming again.

'You can have this room if you like,' Leith was saying. 'I'll take the cupboard at the back.'

Cassie whirled round. 'I'm sorry. I just assumed all the rooms would be like this.' She grinned back. 'I could toss you for it.'

Leith raised an eyebrow, his eyes glinting in the semi-darkness. 'I couldn't possibly deprive you,' he said. 'Not when you like it so much. I don't care where I sleep.'

Immediately the atmosphere between them

thickened and Cassie's pulse started beating a rapid tattoo against her temples. She knew he was thinking of the nights they had shared, squashed together in either her or his single bunk. Not that their surroundings would have changed anything. They had been too obsessed with one another's bodies to care.

'Would you like to take a walk down to the beach before dinner?' Leith asked.

Not really, was the first reply that came to mind—*at least, not with you.* But that response would be childish at best and rude at worst. It wasn't his fault he made her feel like a girl with her first real crush.

'Give me a moment to unpack and freshen up, and I'll meet you in the sitting room. Say, in ten minutes?'

As it was, she was back in five and Leith was already waiting for her.

As they walked down to the powdery white sand and along the shore, Cassie was acutely conscious of Leith walking next to her.

Leith picked up a flat stone and sent it hopping along the water. 'Remind you of anywhere?' he asked.

'Yes,' she whispered. 'Africa.'

'Do you miss it?'

'Yes.' *I miss you, was what she wanted to say.*

'Do you think you'll go back? You haven't said what your plans are when you finish at the practice.'

'The UN is keeping my job open for me. They gave me six months to decide if I could work with them.'

Leith sent a final stone skipping across the water and turned to face her. 'And will you?'

'I—I don't know. I'm not sure if I have the courage.'

He stepped towards her and framed her face with his hands. 'I don't want you to go back, Cassie.'

She almost stopped breathing. She lifted her chin and closed her eyes, expecting, longing to feel his mouth on hers.

But his hands dropped and she felt him step away from her. 'I don't want you to go anywhere I can't be sure you'll be safe, Cassie. No one can say you haven't done your bit.'

Disappointment made her reel. But what had

she been expecting? That Leith would kiss her as if she hadn't run away from him once?

Especially when she knew she was going to run away again.

Back at the house Josie had set a table for two on the deck overlooking the sea. Sadness washed over Cassie. If she were a different person, if she wasn't so scared all the time of being let down, of Leith finding that the person he thought she was didn't really exist, what then? Perhaps there could be a future with Leith? Not that he'd hinted that he still cared. But…but… The way he'd looked at her down on the beach—that wasn't the way a man looked at a friend.

Cassie almost fled to her room in a panic. Could she really spend the next few days with Leith pretending that he didn't set every nerve ending alight?

He pulled her chair out with a flourish. 'Your table awaits, milady.' Judging by his casual manner, he wasn't the least bit affected by her.

Later Cassie couldn't remember what they ate. The sound of the waves against the rocks echoed the beating of her heart. It was as if her world had narrowed until it contained just the two of them. Leith and herself. The way it was meant to be, the way it could never be.

But just for these few nights she was going to push all thoughts of the future away. She would forget about the past, not think of the future. Simply enjoy this short, precious time together.

The next day they were both up early.

Josie had left out a breakfast of fresh fruit and pastries and there was the rich aroma from coffee on the stove.

They sat at the scrubbed kitchen table. Cassie was ravenous. It had to be the sea air, she thought. But there was also this wonderful sense of peace. She hadn't intended to tell Leith about Afghanistan but now that she had she felt lighter than she had in months.

And because he had seen her scars and there was no need to hide her arms from him, she revelled in being able to wear a skimpy halterneck dress over her bikini without feeling self-conscious.

'What are your plans?' Leith said, as he peeled an orange.

'I'm going for a swim,' she said. 'What about you?'

'I think I'll join you,' he said lazily. 'Once I've seen Veronica.'

'I'll wait here for you, if you like. I can't imagine you'll be long.' She swatted a bee away with her hand. 'There's so many of them there must be a nest nearby.'

'Then no doubt we'll be having home-made honey for breakfast some time.'

'So no spiders in your room last night?' she teased. 'I have to admit there was the largest and hairiest one I have ever seen on my ceiling.'

Leith grimaced. 'In that case, I'm very glad I gave you that room. Remind me to send you in tonight to do a recce of mine.'

They grinned at each other and Cassie's heart flipped. She couldn't help it. Everything he said made her remember having sex with him. Whatever else was wrong with her there was clearly nothing wrong with her libido. At least, not since she'd met Leith again.

He gave her another enigmatic smile before excusing himself. Were her lustful thoughts clearly there for him to see?

* * *

Leith had been gone for about half an hour when Cassie heard screaming coming from outside.

She rushed out to find Josie bending over the inert form of a little girl.

'My baby. Tess! Oh, God. Help me,' Josie screamed.

Cassie's heart banged against her ribs. She bent and felt for a pulse. Nothing.

'What happened?' she asked Josie. 'Did she fall? Has she been complaining of feeling unwell?'

'She said a bee stung her. I was just taking the sting out when she said she was itchy all over.' Sure enough, there was a rash on the little girl's body. Cassie hadn't noticed it at first against her darker skin.

Focussed as she was on Josie's daughter, she was only dimly aware of Leith crouching next to her.

'What happened here?' he asked.

'Bee sting. She doesn't have a pulse. I'm assuming anaphylactic shock. Could you fetch my medical bag from my room?'

Leith was on his feet again and within moments he was back. He laid the bag down, opened it and started attaching a bag of fluids to a giving set.

Thank goodness she had brought her emergency paediatric kit with her.

She tried to find a vein, but to her horror they'd collapsed. It sometimes happened when a child's system shut down. It was bad enough in a hospital setting but here, without the right equipment, it could be fatal.

Leith had seen her difficulty and was searching for a vein too but if Cassie with all her experience of children wasn't able to find one then it was unlikely he would fare any better.

Josie was watching them in horrified silence, her little girl's head cradled in her lap.

Everything slowed down again. Just like that day in Afghanistan, Cassie became aware of the sound of crickets, the heat of the sun on her arms, every movement of hers and Leith's happening in slow motion.

Anxiety rose in her throat like bile. She took a deep breath. She had to do something. She simply would not let anyone die because she didn't act soon enough.

Then it came to her. There was another way

to get the fluid into the little girl's veins. Thank God she'd added a couple to her kit.

As Leith monitored Tess's vitals, she rummaged in her medical bag. Right at the bottom was what she was looking for.

'I'm going to use an intraosseous needle to get fluid directly into her circulation,' she told Leith.

'I've heard it can be done,' Leith said quietly, 'although I've never seen it before.'

'It might be better if Mum doesn't stay,' Cassie murmured.

'I'm not leaving my baby,' Josie said fiercely.

'Okay. You need to hold her firmly then, Josie. I'm going to have to push this quite hard—it will look painful—but she won't feel it. Just keep her as still as you can.'

She glanced up and Josie nodded.

Cassie took the needle and using all the strength she could muster forced it directly into the marrow in Tess's bone. When Josie cried out, Cassie was only dimly aware of Leith's voice reassuring her. The procedure looked painful but the child was unconscious and wouldn't feel a thing. As soon as she was certain the needle was in place she started running the saline. A few seconds later, the child stirred.

Cassie felt dizzy with relief. Thank God she hadn't frozen. It was the thing she'd feared most since Afghanistan—that in moments of high stress she'd find herself unable to act. But she'd acted instinctively and had been able to think just as clearly as she'd ever needed to in an emergency. She looked up to find Leith's eyes on her. He nodded slightly. 'Good job,' he said.

'Thanks.' Cassie wanted to appear casual but she couldn't stop smiling. Only another doctor could understand the satisfaction that came with saving a life.

'Now, Josie, Tess is going to be fine. She'll need to be very careful around bees in future and she'll need to carry an EpiPen with adrenaline in it probably for the rest of her life but at least you'll know what to do next time.'

Josie, still pale with shock, nodded. Her little girl opened her eyes and blinked. When she noticed that her mother was crying she started to cry too. It was the sweetest sound. Tess would probably be running around in an hour or two.

'As a precaution, I think we should get her to

the hospital and have her checked out though. They'll also be able to give you a supply of EpiPens and show you how to use them.'

'There is one on the next island. We will have to get a boat.' Josie looked around distractedly. 'My husband is down at the big house.'

Leith was on his feet. 'I'll see what I can organise.'

'I'll go with you to the hospital,' Cassie said to Josie.

'Do you want me to come too?' Leith asked.

'No, thanks. I can take it from here.'

Their eyes caught and held. In his she saw warmth and approval—and something else, something she dare not let herself believe but that made her catch her breath.

'Josie has a lot to thank you for,' he said. 'As soon as I've sorted transport, I'll be right back.'

Veronica offered her small private plane the family used for island hopping to take Cassie, Josie and Tess to the small hospital on the next island. The staff there checked Tess over again, pronounced themselves happy and gave Josie a number of EpiPens to take home with her.

By the time they returned home, most of the adrenaline from earlier had seeped away, but Cassie was still feeling charged up. Leith was waiting for her. At the sight of him, her heart leaped.

'Everything okay?'

She grinned at him. 'Yes.'

In fact, everything was more than okay—everything was perfect. She would have even gone as far as to say she was happy. Somehow over the last few weeks the weight and the darkness that had surrounded her like a fine mist had lifted.

And most of that was down to the man standing in front of her. He was looking particularly pleased about something.

'Veronica and the baby are doing fine,' he said. 'She invited us to lunch, but I took the liberty of declining for both of us. So she suggested we take one of the boats over to one of the uninhabited islands and have lunch there. She asked her cook to pack a picnic lunch for us. What do you say?'

'I say, lead me to it.' Hadn't she decided she was going to throw caution to the wind? So what if there couldn't be a future for her and Leith? So what if there was going to be no happy-ever-after in their story?

They had four days. Soon she'd be leaving the practice and Leith would be out of her life for good. And if she got hurt? That was part of life and suddenly she wanted to feel again, even if feeling meant hurting.

'I'll just grab my stuff,' she said.

The sky was a perfect blue with only wisps of cloud, and the sea was almost translucent. Cassie watched multicoloured fish dart around the boat.

'Veronica's house manager gave me some snorkelling gear,' Leith said. 'I thought we could have a go before lunch.'

'Whatever,' Cassie said, lazily trailing her hand in the cool water. She studied Leith through her lashes. He was bare-chested and his muscles bunched every time he pulled the oars through the water. 'I have to say you row well.'

He grinned back. 'It's not often I get my rowing prowess remarked on. It comes from being brought up on an island. I can't remember a time when I wasn't in, or around, boats. My father took me sailing for the first time when I was five. My mother wouldn't let him take me before that. The seas around Skye can be treacherous if you don't know what you're doing. My father was prone to taking risks, in my mother's opinion. Not that he took too many of those when I was with him. His father was a fisherman and Dad taught me to respect the sea.'

'I can't imagine that we're in much danger here. Even if we do get tipped up, we can practically wade to land.'

Moments later that was what they did. Leith brought the boat as close to the shore as he could, rolled up his cotton trousers to the knee and jumped out. He reached out to Cassie and before she could react had lifted her out of the boat.

As he held her against him she felt the heat radiating from his body, smelled the faint scent of his aftershave, each muscle of his hard body achingly familiar. It felt as if she'd come home. She fought the impulse to wriggle out of his arms with some light remark and instead relaxed as he waded to the beach.

Once there he let her slide to the ground. As

she did she felt the whole length of his body along hers and every cell and synapse seemed to snap to attention.

She laughed shakily and stepped back. She knew what was going to happen, but she wanted to prolong every delicious moment. She wanted to make him want her so much he couldn't think. She cupped his face with her hands and looked into his eyes. His desire for her was plain to see and she revelled in it. This day was hers. Nothing and no one could take it from her.

'What about lunch?' she said huskily.

'Lunch?' He sounded dazed and she suppressed a smile. When he reached out to pull her towards him, she stepped away.

'I think we should eat first and then perhaps a snorkel.'

'You're hungry?' he said disbelievingly.

'Not so much,' she admitted, flicking him a look. Ignoring the way her heart was pounding, she spread the tablecloth on the white sand.

This island, if it were possible, was even more beautiful than the one they'd left. Behind them was a small copse of trees shielding them from view of the other islands and in front fine white sand stretched as far as the eye could see.

Cassie opened the basket as Leith stretched out on the blanket. She remembered every line of his body, every ridge, every muscle, the dark hair on his lower abdomen, the line of his hips. Lust shot through her as she remembered the feel of his hands on her body. She wanted more. She wanted him to be with her for ever. But if she couldn't have that, she wanted this single perfect day.

She laid the fruit out first, acutely aware of Leith's eyes watching her every move. Grapes, Oranges, Mangoes. There was freshly baked bread and salad as well as a bottle of wine. She held it up to Leith with a questioning glance, but he shook his head.

She plucked some grapes from a bunch and, leaning towards him, held them to his mouth. As he caught one between his teeth he reached out for her, but she laughed and moved away.

Keeping her eyes on him, she rolled her hair into a knot on the top of her head and slipped out of her sundress. She was wearing her bikini underneath.

Leith's eyes glinted in the sun and a smile hovered on his lips. 'Do you have any idea what you're doing to me, woman?' he growled.

'Doing to you?' She raised her eyebrows in apparent innocence. 'I'm simply getting ready for a swim.' But she knew her eyes were sparkling. It was good to make him suffer for a while and she wanted to make him suffer for a little longer. Never before had she thought of herself as a seductress but she had to admit she was enjoying the role. Perhaps it was because, just by looking at her, he was making her body feel as if it were on fire. The tension was unbearable.

She stretched, knowing her itsy-bitsy bikini was revealing more than it was concealing. The Brazilian bottom, at which she had baulked at first, somehow now felt so incredibly sexy, so incredibly right. As she bent to pick up her sunscreen she didn't have to hear his muffled groan to know she was turning the screw one more inch. She felt deliciously powerful.

She held out the bottle of sunscreen. 'Would you mind putting some on my shoulders?'

'Come and sit here then,' he said. When he sat up, she positioned herself between his legs with her back towards him. His hands on her skin were cool at first with the cream and she shivered, although she wasn't entirely sure her reaction had anything to do with the temperature of the lotion. He slipped down one strap and then another to expose her shoulders and she sucked in a breath. She didn't know how long she could continue playing this game. The need to feel his hands all over her was so intense she thought she might spontaneously combust there and then.

'Is this okay?' he asked.

She couldn't trust herself to speak so she simply nodded. His hands moved down her back and she trembled under the feel of his strong fingertips. Before she could stop herself she gasped.

'I need to undo the strap at the back if I'm to do the job properly.' His voice had dropped an octave and this time she heard the laughter in *his* voice. She knew he had felt her reaction— heard her small gasp of need and desire—and now he'd turned the tables. He was playing her.

All she could do was nod again and immediately the strap at the back of her bikini was undone and her top was lifted from her shoulders and tossed to one side.

His thumbs traced the ridges of her spine, swept over her shoulders and down along the insides of her arms. His hands stilled where she was scarred. For a moment she wanted to cover herself with her hands but he bent her forward and gently touched each scar with his lips.

She wanted to cry out with the exquisite heat racing along her body but forced herself to stay quiet. Not yet. Not quite yet. She had to hold him away as long as possible. Make the moments last.

Then his hands moved back to her shoulders and he pulled her back until she was leaning against him, the naked skin of her back against his bare chest. Every centimetre of her skin seemed to sizzle where it touched his.

His hands swept up the length of her neck and she had to bite harder on her lip to stop herself from begging him to put an end to her agony. She desperately wanted to turn in his arms so that she could straddle him and have him inside her. But she used every ounce of her resolve to stay where she was. She wasn't going to be the one to break first. She had no doubt that it had turned into a game now and he was much better at it than she was. He was as determined to tease her, to bring her as tantalisingly close to breaking point as she had been to bring him there, and although she no longer believed she was going to win this game, she was determined to hold out as long as possible.

His hands were on her stomach now, his fingertips exploring, touching lightly then harder, swooping down to the top of her bikini bottoms then back to just below her breasts. She couldn't stop herself. She leaned against him and arched her back to encourage him to touch her. She didn't care any more who won this game. She wanted his hands on her—all over her. And she wanted him inside her. Before she exploded.

Then his hands were on her breasts, his thumb and forefinger gently teasing at her nipples. It was no use. She couldn't hold on any longer. She would have to turn and face him. She would have to get him out of his trousers, and the thought of having to wait…

Before she could move, his hands were moving downwards again—across her stomach, gliding gently over the top of her bikini bottom, brushing between her legs and moving on to the tops of her thighs. Instinctively, she parted her legs and his fingers were touching her, gently at first and then with sure, rhythmic strokes. Unable to bear it for one more second, she swivelled round until she was facing him. She unbuttoned his trousers and eased them over his hips, holding his gaze all the while.

Then she reached for him and guided him inside her, where she desperately needed him to be.

Cassie looked up at the clear sky and wondered if she'd ever felt so peaceful—even though soon she and Leith would be parting again.

On the surface, nothing had really changed—Leith had his life and she had hers. But inside everything had changed. Where she'd felt nothing before, now she felt it all, and the pain of loving Leith was the price she was willing pay. But she refused to think about any of that.

They had three days left to be together. Three days that she could pretend were never going to pass. She propped herself up on her elbow and lightly brushed her fingertips across Leith's chest. He opened his eyes and grinned.

When he reached for her she shook her head. 'No,' she whispered, 'this time I'm in control. And I'm going to do to you what you did to me—tease you until you beg.' She climbed on his chest, pinning his arms with her knees. She smiled into his eyes. 'So lie there and let me do the work.'

They'd spent the last three days making love and exploring the island and every night in Cassie's room, their limbs entangled in the sheets, the perspiration on their bodies mingling. It was as if they couldn't get enough of each other. She knew his body now almost as well as she did her own. She loved the feel of his skin under her fingertips, she loved to run her hands over the hard planes of his body and revelled in his response to her.

All too soon it was their last night on the island and, agonisingly, when she wanted to make the most of the last few hours she had with him, they'd had to have dinner with Veronica and her friends—it would have been rude to refuse.

Cassie had been acutely conscious of Leith throughout—without having to look, she would know where he was in the room. Often she would glance up from whoever she'd been talking to and find his eyes on her. And they would share a smile of anticipation, before returning their attention to their hosts. At the first opportunity they got they excused themselves. But to Cassie's surprise—and disappointment—instead of turning up the hill towards their temporary home, Leith suggested a drink down at the pier.

They took a seat at the smallest bar she'd ever seen. It was perched on a jetty, overlooking the crashing waves of the ocean. There was only the barman and one other paying customer, apart from Leith and herself.

The barman poured them their drinks and they took their glasses over to the single table on the edge of the pier.

Cassie leaned back and smiled, enjoying the sensation of the cooling spray from the waves, crashing against the rocks, on her bare legs.

Leith leaned forward and took her hands. 'Do you have any idea how beautiful you are?'

'You're not so bad yourself,' she replied. In fact, he had never seemed more sexy to her. Even in the few days that they had been here, his skin had darkened, emphasising his green eyes and even white teeth.

He looked at her intently. 'We should get married.'

Cassie sucked in her breath. Whatever she'd expected Leith to say, it wasn't this.

'Married?'

'Yes.' He placed his thumb and forefinger under her chin. 'I think we'd be good together.'

'Good together?' Cassie echoed.

'Yes. And Peter likes you. We could be a family.' He grinned. 'Never thought I'd say those words.'

'You think we should get married because Peter likes me?' she said incredulously.

'Well, that and the small matter that I love you and I think you love me.'

Cassie closed her eyes as a wave of happiness washed over her. Did he love her? Truly?

The six-year-old Cassie reared her head. Unlovable. Naughty. Send back. No good.

What did he really know of her now? Almost nothing. But she believed him when he said he loved her. He would never pretend to feel something he didn't.

'We could have more children,' Leith was continuing. 'Brothers and sisters for Peter.'

A shadow fell over her heart.

'But I don't want children, Leith. I can't even see myself as stepmother to Peter.'

As soon as he'd mentioned children, she'd known. Nothing had changed. Children meant pain and sacrifice. And what was worse, she didn't know if she could love a child enough or whether she would love it too much. She might feel better about herself now than she had for as long as she could remember, but that didn't mean she was ready for marriage and children, and deep down she doubted she would ever be.

He frowned. 'I thought you cared about Peter?'

'I do. He's an amazing little boy. But caring for him doesn't mean I could look after him full time. It's different being with a child some of the time to doing the whole mother thing. I don't think I'd be any good at it.'

Leith shook his head. 'I've never met anyone who would make a better mother. I've rushed you. Perhaps you'll change your mind about having children. There's plenty of time.'

'Not so much, Leith. I'm thirty-four, almost

thirty-five. You know more than most what that means for my fertility.'

He came round to her side of the table and pulled her to her feet and into his arms. 'I don't care about your fertility. Just as long as you can love Peter. Whatever fears you have about your ability to mother him, I have none. I want us to be together. For the rest of our lives. Simple.'

'Oh, Leith, it isn't simple at all. Why can't we stay the way we are? We don't need to get married to share our lives.'

'I need us to get married, Cassie,' he murmured into her hair. 'I need to know that you love me and trust me and can't live without me. Or are you saying you don't love me?' He laughed harshly. 'I can't believe that.'

She pulled away until she could look into his eyes. 'Yes, I love you. I never thought I'd ever say those words, but I love you with my heart, my soul, with everything I have.'

'But you won't marry me? At least tell me why.'

She wriggled out of his arms and went to stand at the end of the pier, looking out to sea. Leith came to stand behind her and wrapped his arms around her, holding her so hard she could feel every muscle of his chest against her back. Her heart beat in time with the waves crashing on the shore.

She sighed. 'Remember I told you that I was adopted.'

'Didn't I tell you I remember everything you've ever said? But you didn't tell me much more than that you weren't close to your adoptive parents.'

'It's not something I talk about. I don't see either of my adoptive parents any more. The woman who left me the flat in London was my nanny. She was the person who mothered me in my childhood.'

'Go on,' he said quietly.

'I was removed from my birth mother when I was five—a little younger than Peter is now. Just like Jude with Peter, my mother wasn't able to look after me because she had an addiction problem.' She swallowed.

'It killed her and I was put into care. The woman who eventually adopted me was very like Mrs Forsythe—remember the woman I fell out with? I suspect Lily—my adoptive mother— although I can't think of her as my mother, not even to myself—only adopted me so that she wouldn't stand out as being different from the others in the world she moved in.

'At that time there was such a thing as open adoption, but somehow, I'm not sure how, she must have found out about my birth mother and I think that spoiled me for her. From then on she wanted nothing to do with me. In fact, she made it clear that she would send me back to Social Services if I didn't behave myself. That meant keeping my room immaculate, never questioning her, never speaking unless I was spoken to.

'From the age of eight I was left entirely in the hands of Nanny. Which wasn't so bad. I loved Nanny and I knew she loved me. She tried to explain that it wasn't my fault that Lily didn't love me. She said it was a fault with her own upbringing and not with me and I should always remember that. But children can't really understand. They always think that the fault is with them.

'I tried to be good. So good that she couldn't help but love me, or at least good enough that she wouldn't send me away. Perhaps it would have been better if she had. One good thing came of it, though. Medicine. I studied hard—at first as a way to please Lily and then, when my teachers praised me for always coming top of the class, as a way to feel good about myself.

'School work was never a problem and I suspect the only time Lily was ever proud of me was when I won a place to study medicine at Oxford. She couldn't wait to show me off to her friends then.' She smiled weakly. 'And at least I had Nanny—until I was sent to boarding school when I was eleven.'

Leith growled something under his breath and made to turn her round but she stayed rigid. 'Don't, Leith. If you look at me now I don't know if I'll find it in me to finish my story. And I want you to know everything.

'There was a dreadful fight one day,' she continued. 'I wasn't supposed to hear it, but I always was an inquisitive child. I must have been ten, I think. Nanny and Lily were in the drawing room. I was to go to boarding school, Lily was saying, and Nanny's services would no longer be required.

'Nanny said something about while she didn't approve of boarding school, perhaps in my case it was for the best as I wouldn't have to cope with being brought up by a mother who could hardly look at me and a father who barely seemed to notice I was even part of the household.

'Naturally, that didn't go down very well and Nanny was dismissed.' Cassie blinked. 'But not until I had left for boarding school a couple of months later. It seemed Lily would rather have Nanny and her outspoken views in the house for two more months than have to look after me herself.'

'And your father—Lily's husband?'

'I don't think he was a bad man—just a weak one. I suspect he only agreed to adopt me to keep on the right side of Lily. He was never cruel or unkind to me—but neither did he intervene when Lily was.'

'So that's why you don't see them much?'

'They seem happy not to see me either. They were always finding some reason not to have me home for the school holidays. Nanny—Martha—ended up taking me, which of course suited me just fine. I had become used to Lily's lack of interest in me by this time and to be honest I was happier with Martha.

'Boarding school wasn't really a problem. I

didn't make many friends—I guess I thought there had to be something wrong, something unlovable about me—but I made sure I was well behaved. You won't be surprised to know I continued to do well in all my subjects. I was also head girl. Lily did attend the school functions, however. She liked to be seen by the other parents.

'Anyway, while at university I spent as many summers as I could abroad, either doing locums or any sort of voluntary job I could find. Lily wasn't mean when it came to money. When I wasn't away, I spent time with Nanny. Sometimes Lily didn't even know when I was in London. Then, as soon as I was financially independent, contact tailed off with my adoptive family completely.'

This time he did turn her so she was facing him. 'I have never met anyone more lovable than you. God, Cassie, you're as beautiful on the inside as you are on the outside. Don't you know that?'

'I'm coming to believe it,' she said. 'Being with you…makes me feel good. You make me feel whole in a way I've never felt before. But

I'm still scared I would be useless as a mother. I'm scared I wouldn't be able to love my children enough, or I'd love them too much—in which case I'll probably suffocate them with my love. I know what I'm saying is difficult for you to understand—I don't know if I understand it myself.'

His eyes flickered and she watched his dawning realisation. 'That's why you left me in Africa with only that note, isn't it? Everything was good between us until you found out I had a child.'

She nodded. 'I knew it wouldn't be fair to let you believe there could be a future for us. Not when you had Peter in your life.'

'But that's crazy. He loves you. And you love him. You're not Lily. You could never be her.'

'I know. At least, I know in my head that the way I feel isn't rational, but I can't seem to talk myself out of it.'

'So what are you saying, Cassie?' A muscle twitched in his jaw. 'Don't ask me to choose between you and Peter, because I won't. No matter how much I love you, I won't give up my son.'

She touched his face with her fingers, imprinting the memory of him into her pores. 'I know. You wouldn't be the man I love if you did.'

He placed his hands on either side of her face and smiled wryly. 'I've waited this long to find the woman I want to spend the rest of my life with, so I guess I can wait a bit longer.'

He rubbed his thumb along the line of her jaw. 'But, my darling love, please don't make me wait too long.'

That night, as he lay with Cassie in his arms, Leith thought about what she'd told him. It explained so much—her fear of loving and being loved, of becoming a mother, her lack of trust.

Of course he wasn't looking for a mother for Peter—he just wanted Peter's natural mother to be well enough to care for their son the way he needed to be cared for. But whatever Cassie thought, she would make an outstanding, loving mother. Peter, as he'd told her, had already fallen under her spell.

He gazed down at her. His chest tightened as he saw that in sleep she had a smile on her lips. Over the last weeks the bruise-like shadows under her eyes had disappeared and more and more often he'd see her eyes light up and hear the laugh he loved so much.

It would take time to peel back all the layers that made up the woman he adored. If only she could believe that her heart was good. The lines of a poem came back to him. Didn't she know he would never tread on her heart?

But he wouldn't abandon his child. Not even for her. He loved them both and he had to believe that Cassie would come to trust his love for her.

Until then, he would wait.

The next morning, Cassie woke to an empty bed. Knowing that Leith was probably down at the main house, seeing Veronica, she went into the garden to pick some oranges to squeeze for breakfast. She'd only been there for a few minutes when Josie came in search of her.

'Dr Leith wants you at the house.'

Immediately Cassie knew there was something wrong. She picked up her bag and hurried down the narrow path to where Veronica and her party were staying.

A grim-looking Leith met her in the hall. 'I checked the baby's heartbeat as usual. Up until today it's been fine, but I think you should check it too. It seems to be really slow—about sixty beats per minute. I checked Veronica's pulse in case that's what I was hearing, but hers is a bit faster than usual—probably from anxiety.'

'Sure,' said Cassie, mentally running through the reasons the baby's heart rate could have dipped. None, in her experience, was likely to be good news.

'I've put Veronica's pilot on alert,' Leith said. 'We should get her to hospital in case I have to deliver her.'

'God, Leith, she's only just thirty-two weeks.'

He rubbed his chin. 'I know. It's only a precaution at the moment.'

Veronica was waiting for them in her bedroom.

'Hi, Veronica,' Cassie greeted the anxious-looking woman calmly. 'Leith has asked me to listen to the baby's heart. Would that be okay?'

As soon as she heard the slow beating of the baby's heart she knew Leith had been right to call her. The baby was still moving so that was good but, nevertheless, they had to get Veronica to hospital—and as soon as possible.

* * *

A few hours later Veronica was lying in a hospital bed looking pale and frightened. Leith and Cassie had consulted with the local doctors and following several scans and tests now had their diagnosis. It had been agreed that Leith and Cassie would be the ones to tell Veronica their diagnosis.

Cassie sat down next to Veronica and took her hand while Leith remained standing at the foot of the bed.

'The first thing you need to know is that there is every chance your baby is going to be fine, Veronica,' Cassie began. 'So you mustn't panic when you hear what we have to say.'

'But something is wrong, isn't it?' Veronica's voice was thin with fear.

'Yes. Your baby's heart rate slowed suddenly. This can be caused by a number of things, which is why we wanted you in hospital.'

'Is she going to be all right?'

'We think she has a heart condition—that's why we've been doing all these scans. But looking at the scan, your baby's heart looks normal—she has all the usual chambers and connections to all the important blood vessels—and we can't see any holes in her heart or other abnormalities. So we wondered if the problem could be a heart block—that's where the electrical signals through the heart aren't being conducted as usual, causing the heart to pump more slowly than usual.

'We've also ordered some more blood tests in case there are antibodies in your blood that is causing heart block in the baby.'

'What does all that mean?' Veronica cried. 'I don't understand.'

'It means it's likely that she will have to be delivered early by Caesarean and may need an operation, but...' Cassie rushed on as Veronica blanched, 'I have seen many babies with the same condition grow into healthy children and know of many more that have grown into healthy adults. I know all this sounds scary but we will make sure that you have the best cardiologists looking after you.

'You'll need regular scans to check that the baby is still growing and you'll need to be delivered in a hospital where there are specialist paediatric heart surgeons. At delivery we'll check that baby is okay and she'll be monitored closely until we can tell whether she'll need a pacemaker.

'If the baby appears unwell at birth, we may put in a pacemaker as an emergency just to be on the safe side. Sometimes it's not possible to tell until some time after the baby is born. I know this is a lot to take in, but we'll go over it as many times as you need. In the meantime—although I know it's hard—try not to worry.'

'Why wasn't this picked up before? You did my last scan, Leith, and you said everything was normal.'

'It was, Veronica,' Leith replied. 'These things often only become apparent later on in pregnancy.'

'So what now?'

Cassie could see that Veronica was determined not to cry.

'There's nothing that can be done until your baby is big enough to be safe to deliver her.'

'I want to go home to England. I want my mother. I need her with me.' Frightened eyes held Cassie's. 'Please let me go to her.'

Leith and Cassie looked at one another. Cassie

nodded. While she wouldn't usually recommend travelling, it couldn't hurt the baby and it could only help Veronica if she was close to home. Her heart tightened as she recognised Veronica's desperate need to be with her mother. That's what a mother and daughter relationship should be like.

'I could try and organise an air ambulance to take you,' she offered.

Veronica sagged against the pillow, as relief replaced the anxiety in her eyes. She shook her head. 'No need. My husband will organise our private plane for me.' She looked at Cassie and Leith and her mouth trembled. 'You'll both stay with me until I get home?'

'Of course,' Cassie said. 'We'll be with you every step of the way.'

CHAPTER ELEVEN

Cassie stood next to Leith looking down at the tiny newborn. Veronica was sitting beside the incubator, her face white with anxiety.

'She's so small to be needing an operation,' she whispered.

'They're very good here,' Cassie said. 'She couldn't be in safer hands.' As they'd suspected, Veronica's daughter did need a pacemaker. However, the paediatric heart surgeons were optimistic that the little girl would go on to lead a happy and productive life.

But looking down at the tiny form, Cassie was reminded once more why she couldn't bear to have children. Loving brought nothing but pain and terror.

They left the new mother with her baby and stepped outside. Summer was almost over and soon Cassie would be leaving the practice.

It was as if Leith had read her thoughts. 'Would

you come with Peter and I to Skye after you finish here?' he asked.

Leith and Peter were to spend the last couple of weeks of the school holidays on Skye. Apparently Peter was desperate to go back.

'I'm not sure that's a good idea.'

He cupped her chin with the palm of his hand. 'Say yes. Please.'

She shook her head as tiny shards of ice pierced her heart. Nothing had changed. She loved Leith but she couldn't be the woman he wanted—the woman he and little Peter deserved.

'For God's sake, Cassie, what do I have to do to convince you that I love you? That you'll be safe with me? That I'll never stop loving you?' He placed his hands on either side of her face and she couldn't stop herself from kissing the soft pad of his hand.

Her throat was tight and she knew tears weren't far away. 'There's nothing you can say or do. Forget about me, Leith.'

As she turned to leave he grabbed her by the arm. His eyes had softened. 'You know that's not going to happen. I know you love me. And Peter. All I need is for you to trust me.' He touched her lips with his fingertips. 'Trust me, Cassie. Trust my love. We can be a family—the three of us.' He dropped a kiss on her forehead. 'And when you come to believe that, I'll be waiting. However long it takes.'

In the days that followed, Cassie couldn't stop thinking about Leith and his proposal. Why couldn't she trust him enough to believe that he would never stop loving her? Why couldn't she trust herself enough to believe she could be a good wife and mother? Why couldn't she trust him enough to believe him when he said she and Peter were enough for him?

What was wrong with her? She knew that her adoptive parents' attitude towards her had been wrong. Hundreds of children grew up unloved yet managed to make loving, supportive parents. At least, she knew that on an intellectual level. Deep inside she still felt like the same unlovable child.

But Leith had said he would give her time. There was no hurry. They could carry on as they were. Katie had given birth to a baby boy two weeks ago while Leith and Cassie had been in the Caribbean. Fabio would be coming back from leave soon and she'd no longer be needed.

She finished her morning clinic. There was nothing too worrying, just the usual sore throats and immunisations. She had a home visit that afternoon to a little boy who wasn't developing as fast as his mother thought he should be. The mother had offered to bring the child to the practice, but Cassie thought it would be better to see him in his home environment.

In the meantime, she needed some coffee and a sandwich. And, she admitted to herself with a smile, if she caught sight of Leith, that would be a bonus.

Katie was in Reception, showing off Marcus, her new baby, to Rose and the nurses. The new mother was glowing as she basked in the admiration of the staff.

Knowing it was expected of her, Cassie stepped forward to add her congratulations.

She had to admit he really was the cutest baby with his button nose and shock of dark brown hair.

'Would you mind holding him for me?' Katie

asked as the others melted away. 'I need to visit the ladies.'

Before Cassie could say anything, Katie had passed her the small bundle wrapped tightly in his blanket.

A pair of brown eyes stared up into hers.

'Hello,' Cassie whispered.

Marcus brought a tiny fist up towards Cassie's face and the little fingers grasped her finger with surprising strength. Something inside her shifted.

What would it be like to be responsible for this life for the rest of your own life? To know that whatever happened your life was inextricably linked with another's? To live in fear every day that you might not be a good enough mother— that because of you your child might grow up broken inside? It was such a responsibility. Little Marcus yawned and burped. Just then a warmth spread through her, bringing with it a longing so intense it almost made her cry out loud.

Katie came back from the ladies. 'Let me take him.' When she passed Marcus across Cassie felt bereft. Dear God, what was she going to do?

CHAPTER TWELVE

LEITH AND PETER left for Skye the next day. Their leaving hurt more than she could have ever thought possible. By the time they returned she'd be gone.

Leith's goodbye was cool, almost as if he was taking his leave of a stranger. And who could blame him?

Before he left he'd slipped a note into her hand. She hadn't read it yet. What was the point? Unexpectedly, the thought of never seeing Peter again made her heart splinter into tiny pieces. It was almost as bad as knowing that she wouldn't see Leith again. Her days would be so dark without him. Without them both.

She stared out of the window of the flat. Summer was all but over and the new owners would be moving in at the end of the month. Turning the note over in her hand, she noticed for the first time that the writing of her name on the front of the envelope wasn't in Leith's hand. The large block letters, along with the misspelling of her name, could only belong to one person.

She tore open the envelope and read.

Dear Casy
Please come to sky. I miss you. I made a
wish. You promised.
Peter.

The letter fell from her fingers. What an idiot she'd been. As Leith had said, Peter already loved her. How could she walk away from him now? How could that be better for him?

She loved Peter. She would never stop loving the little boy, just as she would never stop loving Leith. She might not always be a perfect mother, but didn't she owe it to them—to herself—to try?

And if she stumbled along the way, Leith would be ready to catch her. Catch them both. Keep them safe. Love them. No matter what.

It was Saturday morning by the time Cassie made it to Staffin. She would have tried to make it last night but she'd been held up. The practice had thrown her a small party. The gesture had touched her more than she would have thought possible. Once more she'd allowed herself to get close to people. They had become her family, but this time it was different. She didn't feel that she had to keep up a façade. They knew her and still cared about her.

Now it was time to see Leith and Peter. How could she have almost let her chance of happiness slip away? She didn't have to be the best wife and mother in the world. All she had to do was the best she could. And to love. And, God, did she love.

As her car pulled up at Leith's parents' house she saw he was digging in the garden, a small figure beside him mimicking every move. They both had their shirts off and were wearing jeans. There couldn't be any doubt whose child Peter was.

Behind them, Leith's mother was feeding the chickens.

When Leith looked up his face broke into a wide smile and her heart leaped. She would never love anyone the way she loved this man.

Peter threw down his spade and ran towards her, flinging his small arms around her legs and almost knocking her off her feet with the ferocity of his grip. 'You came! My wish came true!'

'Hey, Peter,' she said, hunkering down. 'It's great to see you.' She loved Leith's son as much as she loved Leith. With Leith by her side, how could she fail? How had it taken all this time for her to realise that she wasn't like Lily? Leith and Peter wouldn't stop loving her if she wasn't perfect.

'Come and see my chickens,' Peter said, taking her by the hand. 'My dad says they're mine to keep. All mine.'

He beamed up at her and there was no sign of the pale, troubled boy she'd first met. When she looked at Leith, his grin got wider. She knew what having Peter's trust and love meant to him.

Taking Peter by the hand, she let him drag her over to where his chickens were. Five tiny yellow chicks were huddled together in a little nest made of straw. Peter pointed out each one by name, although Cassie had to wonder how he could tell any of the identical chicks apart.

'I wanted to take them home to our house in

London with me,' Peter said, 'but Daddy says it's cruel to take them away from their mum until they get older.' He looked up at Cassie. 'He says they only took me away from my mum until she gets better and can look after me again. Soon, if I want, I can go and live with her when I'm not with him.'

Cassie looked up at Leith in surprise and raised one eyebrow in a silent question.

She moved away from Peter, who was crouched next to his little chicks and watching over them like any proud father.

'Apparently she's doing well,' Leith said. 'Bella says that Jude'll be leaving the clinic soon and she plans to move in with her and Peter. So I don't see any reason why he can't go back to live with Jude some of the time. As long as she keeps well, that is.' He looked over at his son. 'She's determined to stay well for Peter and I believe her. In the end, only time will tell, but I'm optimistic.'

'That's wonderful news. And to see Peter so content... It must make you so relieved.'

Leith grinned. 'I never thought I'd enjoy being

a dad so much. Now there's only one thing missing from my life.'

As he looked into her eyes, Cassie thought her heart would leap out of her chest. 'Cassie...' But before he could say anything more, Peter had run over to them and flung himself into his arms.

'Now Cassie is here, can we go back to the Fairy Glen, Dad? I want to see if there are any fairies about.'

'I don't think the fairies like to be seen, son, but, yes, of course we can go. That is, if Cassie would like to...?'

From the look in his eyes Cassie suspected that wasn't all he was asking. She held her breath. How could she have ever believed that she could live without this man for the rest of her life? A man who had waited, with the patience of a saint, for her to trust him. Finally she knew without a shadow of doubt that she would love him and his son the way they deserved to be loved, just as she knew they would always love her.

With Leith by her side she could do anything. At last she was ready to take a chance on love. As her heart swelled, she smiled. 'Silly Daddy, doesn't he know that fairy-tales can come true?'

Leith looked at her and she read the question in his eyes. She held the gaze of the man who had become her life. 'Wherever you and your dad go, Peter,' she promised softly, 'I'm coming too.'

Six months later Cassie stood next to Leith outside Dunvegan Castle. It had seemed the natural spot for their wedding. Peter was running around in his smart new suit that had been made especially for him to wear as pageboy. No doubt it would be ruined. But Cassie didn't care. She adored her stepson and, in eight months, he would have a little brother or sister. Although she was looking forward to the baby, she wouldn't love Peter any less. He was as much her child now as he was Leith's.

Sometimes in the night she still woke up feeling anxious and panicky, but Leith was always there to hold her and to hush her back to sleep. He knew that her fears and anxieties were part of her and he had promised to spend the rest of his life making sure she knew that she was loved and treasured.

She looked into the eyes of the man she loved more than life itself. She had nearly lost him twice but she would never, ever lose him again. Whatever happened, Leith, her darling husband, would be there by her side, and she by his.

She had her fairy-tale ending after all.

* * * * *

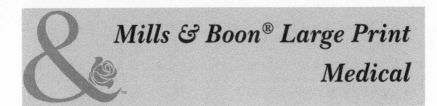

Mills & Boon® Large Print Medical

November

December

January

Mills & Boon® Large Print

Medical

February

March

April